"All men aren't bad.

"I know I'm not a stinker," Madison said.

"Oh, really? Gosh, let me look at you. You're very rare indeed."

"Claire, you're really not that cynical, are you?"

The corners of her mouth lifted in a wry smile. "Not cynical, just smart."

"You can't be a man hater."

"On the contrary. I like men, as long as they're this far away." She indicated the width of the table between them.

"You're playing it too safe. Nothing can happen at that distance."

She laughed softly. "That's the whole point, Mr. McCrea."

Without warning, he came around the table to where she was and reached for her hand. "How about this distance? Don't you think this is much nicer?"

Dear Reader,

Welcome to Silhouette Romance—experience the magic of the wonderful world where two people fall in love. Meet heroines who will make you cheer for their happiness, and heroes (be they the boy next door or a handsome, mysterious stranger) who will win your heart. Silhouette Romance novels reflect the magic of love—sweeping you away with books that will make you laugh and cry, heartwarming, poignant stories that will move you time and time again.

In the next few months, we're publishing romances by many of your all-time favorites such as Diana Palmer, Brittany Young, Annette Broadrick and many others. Your response to these authors and other authors in Silhouette Romance has served as a touchstone for us, and we're pleased to bring you more books with Silhouette's distinctive medley of charm, wit and—above all—*romance*.

During 1991, we have many special events planned. Don't miss our WRITTEN IN THE STARS series. Each month in 1991, we're proud to present readers with a book that focuses on the hero—and his astrological sign.

I hope you'll enjoy this book and all of the stories to come. Come home to romance—Silhouette Romance—for always!

Sincerely,

Tara Gavin
Senior Editor

STELLA BAGWELL

A Practical Man

Published by Silhouette Books New York

America's Publisher of Contemporary Romance

To Beth,
my editor and dear friend.

SILHOUETTE BOOKS
300 E. 42nd St., New York, N.Y. 10017

A PRACTICAL MAN

ISBN: 0-373-08789-6

First Silhouette Books printing April 1991

Books by Stella Bagwell

Silhouette Romance

Golden Glory #469
Moonlight Bandit #485
A Mist on the Mountain #510
Madeleine's Song #543
The Outsider #560
The New Kid in Town #587
Cactus Rose #621
Hillbilly Heart #634
Teach Me #657
The White Night #674
No Horsing Around #699
That Southern Touch #723
Gentle as a Lamb #748
A Practical Man #789

STELLA BAGWELL

lives with her husband and teenage son in southeastern Oklahoma, where she says the weather is extreme and the people are friendly. When she isn't writing romances, she enjoys horse racing and touring the countryside on a motorcycle.

Stella is very proud to know that she can give joy to others through her books. And now, thanks to the Oklahoma Library for the Blind in Oklahoma City, she is able to reach an even bigger audience. The library has transcribed her novels onto cassette tapes so that blind people across the state can also enjoy them.

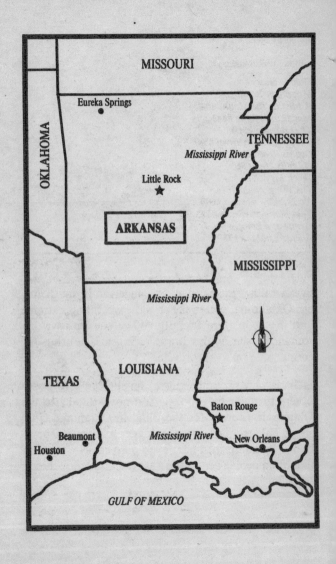

Chapter One

Madison McCrea pulled the company pickup safely to the side of the steep road and pushed on the emergency brake. He didn't think there was a level spot to be found in Eureka Springs. If there was, it was as rare as a room for rent.

He removed his yellow hard hat and placed it on the seat beside him, then looked out the window at the old Victorian-type house perched on the hillside. It wasn't as well-kept or fancy as many of the old homes downtown. But that suited Madison just fine. He hated the sound of traffic when he was trying to sleep and fancy was not his style.

He climbed out of the truck and walked down the narrow sidewalk to the front porch. There was no sign hanging out that proclaimed the place to be a bed-and-breakfast, nor that it had a room for rent. Still, the man he'd been dealing with at the lumberyard assured him it was the best place to stay.

It was a little past one o'clock and Madison was hungry. He hadn't taken time to eat breakfast and now that lunch had rolled around, he'd decided he'd better find a room before he did anything else. For the past week, he'd been stuck on the building site in the tiny camper that he normally used as an office. The narrow walls were beginning to close in on him.

After knocking on the door, he turned around and made a quick survey of the yard as he waited for an answer. Red and purple petunias grew in borders near the house. The porch was filled with hanging ferns, flowering begonias and impatiens. The right side of the house was shaded by a huge sweet gum tree. Beneath it a group of white wrought iron chairs were gathered next to a matching round table.

The grass was neatly mowed and purple martins chirped and called from a nearby birdhouse. He took a deep sigh and prayed a room would be available.

"Could I help you?"

Madison whirled around at the feminine voice to find a lovely woman standing before him. "Yes, you can. I heard you had a room for rent."

He was aware of her eyes looking him over and for the first time in a long while Madison felt a blush creeping up his neck.

"Yes, I do have a room."

Her voice was low, husky and went perfectly with the rest of her. He figured she was in her thirties but it was very difficult to tell which half. Her dark brown hair was long, inching past her shoulders. It waved and curled in gentle layers about her head and had a tousled, sexy look.

At the moment she was shaking it back from her eyes and he caught the flash of long golden earrings against her neck. There was something about her that made him feel like a teenager. He realized he was staring, yet he couldn't seem to do a thing about it.

She extended her hand to him. "My name is Claire Deupree. Would you like to come in so we could discuss this more comfortably?"

Madison took her hand, finding it soft and warm. "Yes, thank you," he said. "My name is Madison McCrea. I'm from—"

"East Texas?" she asked.

His brows lifted as he reluctantly let go of her hand. "Beaumont, ma'am. How did you know?"

A faint smile touched her lips. Lips that Madison was certain God had purposely made for kissing. They were full and pouty and a dusky pink color that brought his thoughts to other things and had his eyes slipping down to the thrust of her breasts.

"I used to live in Baton Rouge," she explained, turning and entering the house.

Madison followed her.

"As you can see, the place is not grand. Have you tried some of the other bed-and-breakfasts in town?"

"A couple. They weren't what I was looking for."

Madison felt more than saw the comfortable room around him. His eyes were on Claire Deupree's backside. She was wearing a pair of jeans, the kind that had been washed with bleach or rocks or whatever to make them white. The denim clung to her bottom like a glove and the movement of her body as she walked was causing all sorts of erotic thoughts to run through his mind.

Claire turned around to face him, motioning for him to take a seat on a chintz couch.

"And what are you looking for, Mr. McCrea?"

She ended the question with a smile. Before he knew what he was doing, Madison was smiling back at her and settling himself on the couch as if he had all day instead of the thirty minutes he'd alloted himself for finding a room and grabbing a sandwich somewhere for lunch.

"Something quiet and homey."

Claire smiled again as she discreetly sized up the man in front of her. He was young. Thirty at the most, she decided. Tall, lean and muscular, he had the look of a man who worked and played hard. Definitely not the quiet, homey sort. His face had a lean, angular look that made his jawline and cheekbones prominent. Warm brown hair, streaked by the sun, waved casually about his head. She suspected it had once been cut short, but he'd obviously neglected to visit the barbershop. It dipped with abandon over his ears and curled against the back of his neck. There was a faint stubbornness to his chin, and a subtle sensuality about his thin lips. The deep cleft above them led up to a strong, straight nose.

All these things she noticed about him in one sweeping glance. But mostly she noticed his eyes. They were dark blue and fringed with thick brown lashes. Their color reminded her of a sapphire ring she owned. Claire loved sapphires. Too bad she wasn't as fond of men, because this one was darling to look at.

"Are you planning on staying long, Mr. McCrea?"

"It all depends on how things go with the weather."

"Well, does that mean two nights, three nights, a week?"

He chuckled because she thought he was a tourist and rightly so, he supposed. Eureka Springs was strictly a tourist town. "No, more like six or eight weeks. I'm constructing a new sixty-unit motel on the south side of town."

Claire looked at him, considering. He was constructing a motel? He certainly looked too young to be a boss of that sort. "Oh, I see. May I ask who told you about my place? I don't advertise because I only have two rooms, and I'm choosy as to who I let in my home."

"That's understandable. Lester down at the lumberyard suggested trying you."

Madison reached to his back pocket and pulled out a leather wallet. Claire watched him search through the contents. After a moment he handed her several cards.

"There's some identification if you need it."

Claire didn't really need it, not if Lester sent him her way. However, she made a point of glancing over the cards. "McCrea Construction," she read aloud. "Is that you?"

He nodded. "We used to work only in the Beaumont area, but things began to expand."

She handed him back the cards. "You own the company?"

Madison shoved the wallet back into his jeans. "That's right."

"You seem very young." Claire didn't know why she'd said that; it just seemed to slip out. She hoped he didn't take offense because it hadn't meant to be a put-down. It was merely an observation.

He grinned at her. "You don't have to be old to know what you're doing."

Claire's mouth twitched. "That might depend on what you're trying to do. But as for the room, it's yours if you want it. Your rent will also include breakfast and supper. Of course I do all the linens, but you'll have to take care of your own laundry."

He nodded. "What about a telephone in the room?"

"Right beside the bed." She gave him the number and he quickly jotted it on a small scrap of paper and stuffed it into his shirt pocket. "It's just an extension," she went on, "not a separate number. So if you make long distance calls, please keep up with them."

"No problem. I'll be using my calling card." He rose to his feet, smoothing his hands down the front of his jeans. "If it's all right with you, I'll sign the lease this evening. Right now I'm running late."

Surprised, Claire also rose to her feet. "You don't want to see the room first?"

Shaking his head, he said, "There's no need. I can tell just by looking at this room that it will be fine."

Claire shrugged as she walked with him back to the front entrance. "I wouldn't want you to be disappointed," she explained.

"I can assure you I won't be." He stepped out onto the porch and reached for her hand. "Thank you, Miss Deupree."

Before she could make a reply he'd dropped her hand and was striding quickly down the sidewalk toward a white pickup with the words McCrea Construction written on the side.

She watched him until he climbed behind the wheel of the pickup. Then she turned and went back into the house before he started the motor and pulled away.

Claire went to the kitchen, which was down a narrow hall past the staircase, and situated at the back of the house. There was a large screened-in porch built onto it and it was here that Claire served all the meals, as long as weather permitted. There was a dining room that could be used when the weather was bad, but even then Claire rarely used it. When there was snow and rain and cold, Claire served her guests and friends in the big kitchen where there was a long pine table with benches on either side. She liked her home warm and casual and that was the way she tried to make it for those around her.

She'd been preparing a salad for lunch when Madison McCrea had knocked on the door. Now she quickly went to work with the remaining ingredients, then poured herself a glass of iced tea to go with it.

The front door banged and a loud sniffling noise sounded just as Claire was carrying her lunch out to the back porch. She sat down and began to munch her salad, knowing that Liv would appear in the doorway any minute.

"Claire, are you busy, dear?"

Claire looked up to see the small, white-headed woman. Liv was in her late sixties and had been a widow for the past five years. She was actually from Illinois, but six months ago she'd come to Eureka Springs as a tourist. Now she didn't intend to leave. She'd made her home here with Claire and apparently liked it. Until she had a row with Arthur.

"Just having lunch, Liv. Would you like something?"

"No thank you, Claire. I had a sandwich earlier at the club."

The club meant a restored old home where senior citizens got together for meals, card games, dancing or just plain socializing.

Liv sat down in a chair across from Claire and crossed her slender legs. She was wearing white walking shorts, a bright red blouse and matching red socks with white tennis shoes. She was in terrific shape for her age. Even though the passing years had dimmed the delicate beauty of her face, it was still there for anyone who took the time to notice.

"So, what's up? Have you and Arthur been at it again?"

Liv sniffed loudly and dabbed a dainty handerchief at her eyes. "The man is a lothario, Claire! I'm never going to speak to him again!"

Claire sipped her tea. "You've said that before, Liv."

"But this time I mean it!"

Liv's blue eyes were blazing and Claire had to duck her head to hide the smile on her face. It wasn't that she didn't feel for the woman. Claire had actually grown very fond of her. But she couldn't help but be amused at Liv's passionate outbursts when it came to Arthur.

"So what has he done now? I thought you two had a lovely time yesterday."

"We did! But that was because there were no other women around."

"Oh, I take it there were other women around today?"

Liv nodded as Claire continued to eat her salad.

"As soon as I walked in the door, there was Arthur dancing in the arms of that . . . that trollop Ruthann."

"You mean the redheaded lady who owns the antique store downtown?"

"Antiques, my foot!" Liv snorted. "She wouldn't know an antique if it whopped her between the eyes."

Claire chuckled in spite of the infuriated look on her friend's face. "I think you're making far more out of this than it really is, Liv. I've seen how Arthur looks at you when he comes over."

"Of course you would think that. He looks at me with that same gleam in his eye that he has for every other woman in his sight!" With a frustrated snort, Liv rose from the chair. "I'm going up to my room. I don't even want to think about Arthur or any man."

"Oh, Liv, speaking of men, we'll be having a new boarder, starting tonight," Claire told the woman before she headed back into the house.

"A man?"

Claire nodded as she recalled the strong image of Madison McCrea. "Yes, he's a building contractor."

"Will he be staying long?"

"Six or eight weeks, he says."

Liv suddenly looked interested. "Really? Is he rich? Good-looking? How old is he?"

"Liv! You were just shedding tears over Arthur."

"Well," she huffed, drawing up all five feet of her. "Arthur's not the only fish in the pond you know."

"Mr. McCrea is probably thirty-five years younger than Arthur, but who knows? He might just like older women."

Liv laughed saucily and left Claire to finish her lunch alone.

After she cleaned her dishes, she climbed the stairs to put fresh linens on Madison McCrea's bed.

The bedrooms were all on the second floor. Claire's and Liv's were situated at the front of the house over the living room. Madison McCrea's was across the hall at the back. It had two windows. One faced north and the side of the hill that had an orchard of fruit trees and grapevines. The other faced the back, which looked out over a deep wooded valley that disappeared into the mountains. There was a peaceful beauty to the view and she wondered if Madison McCrea was a man to notice such things.

Her thoughts continued along the same line as she pulled the pale green comforter off the four-poster and began to stretch a sheet across the mattress. More than likely the man would be the kind who worked long hours and never took the time to notice anything. He'd probably just use the room to sleep and shower, nothing more, Claire decided.

Still, she took special care to see that his private bathroom was spotlessly clean with plenty of towels and soap, that there were extra blankets at the foot of the bed in case the night grew chilly, and that the heavy wooden dresser and chest were free of dust, the drawers smelling of fresh potpourri. She even switched on the portable TV sitting in one corner to make sure it was working properly.

Claire went through the same routine with each new guest. But somehow this time was different. As she fussed around the room, she kept seeing Madison McCrea's face and remembering the way he'd smiled at her.

Just for a moment his blue eyes had caused her heart to skip a beat. And that was very unusual for Claire. She might go out with a man once in a while just for casual company, but she had never allowed one to dominate her thoughts, and she certainly wasn't about to let it happen in the future.

It was raining when Madison McCrea returned. Claire was in the kitchen preparing pork chops for the evening meal when she heard the sound of a truck outside.

Wiping her hands on a dish towel, she made her way to the front of the house. Through the screen door, she watched him stride down the sidewalk. He was wearing a yellow rain slicker, which was smeared in several places with mud and grease. His boots were also caked with mud. Rain was dampening his hair and the piece of luggage he was carrying.

"Hello, Mr. McCrea. I see you made it back."

Her voice was still just as warm and husky as he'd remembered it from earlier that day. She was holding the door open for him and suddenly he didn't feel nearly as tired as he had a few minutes ago.

"I'm a muddy mess, ma'am. You'd better let me take off my boots and slicker here on the porch."

"Don't worry about the floors. They're hardwood and moppable," she assured him. She'd never had a workingman stay in her home before. But she'd once been a waitress in a truck stop and she'd quickly learned to deal with grease and grime. Besides, this man seemed to be thoughtful and she didn't want him thinking she was fastidious. She wanted to make him feel relaxed and welcome, as she did all her guests.

"My Mama didn't raise me that way," he told her, setting his bag aside so that he could tug off his boots.

Claire promptly picked up his bag while he shed his boots and slicker.

"I'll carry your things. Just follow me up the stairs," she told him.

Madison walked behind her, his stockinged feet soundless as they made their way across the living room.

"It's nasty out there. We finally had to quit for the day," he said.

She glanced back over her shoulder at him. "You mean this isn't the regular time you'll be arriving?"

"No. I try to make use of all the daylight hours. It will probably be eight or eight-thirty most days. Why? Does that pose a problem?"

"Of course not. I'll just save your supper and heat it in the microwave."

"You shouldn't worry yourself about feeding me. I'm a lone wolf. I pick up scraps here and there."

"It's no worry. Your meals are part of the deal. I'd like for you to enjoy them."

Madison watched the sway of her hips as she climbed the narrow staircase. She was still wearing the same blue jeans, but she'd changed her shirt. This one was white and silky with the sleeves rolled up on her forearms. Her dark hair was caught up on the back of her head in a red barrette and red lipstick stained her lips. There was a sultriness about her that Madison couldn't ignore and with each passing moment he was finding it more and more difficult to keep his mind on the business at hand.

"That's kind of you, ma'am," he said.

"Please call me Claire. I'd like for you to."

"As long as you call me Madison."

"Madison it is, then."

At the landing Claire turned to the right. "Your room is across from mine and Liv's. She's my other guest. Although since she's been here for six months now, I think of her as a friend."

"Do your guests usually stay that long?" Madison asked as he followed her into the room.

"No. Usually two or three nights. A week at the most. You and Liv are the exception."

She set down his bag beside the bed, then turned to him with a questioning look. "Well, what do you think?"

Madison thought he'd died and gone to heaven. He couldn't imagine anything better than coming home each evening and finding her here. "About what?" he asked, his eyes on her face as he rubbed both hands over his damp hair.

Claire's dark brows drew together in a puzzled frown. "About the room. Is it okay?"

He forced himself to look around. It was spacious, very clean and seemed to have everything a person could need. He nodded. "It's nice. Very nice."

She smiled warmly, then crossed over to the windows to look out at the mountains. "The view is particularly lovely from here. When this house first became mine I stayed in this room, but after I started renting out to guests I thought it was selfish of me. So I moved across the hall."

He walked toward her and the windows. "Why should you feel selfish?"

Shrugging, she pulled aside the curtains so that he could see the scenery. "Because I live here, I can enjoy a view of the mountains anytime. A tourist only has but a few days."

Madison leaned his shoulder against the window jamb and looked out. He agreed it was a beautiful sight. Variegated shades of green layered the mountains, each color growing darker as it veed into a network of narrow valleys. Closer to the house was an open meadow, which he supposed somone used for grazing or haying. To the left, where the backyard broke away into the woods, he could see the beginning of an orchard growing along the steep hillside.

"Living in Beaumont I'm not used to seeing mountains like this. It's a change." He turned away from the window to look at her. She wasn't short, nor was she tall. Her chin would probably strike the middle of his chest. At the moment her head was tilted backward as she looked up at him. "You must be a generous person, giving up this room."

She laughed softly, as if the idea of her being generous came as a surprise. "Maybe you won't think that when I tell you the rent."

Madison knew that whatever it was, it would be worth it. Just seeing her face each evening would make it so. Madison liked women. Some of the people he considered his very best friends were women. And then there'd been others he'd been enamored with for varied amounts of time. But there was something about this one that shook him awake. She was different. He didn't know why and he didn't know what was telling him that she was, but he knew it just the same.

When she stated the amount, he replied, "That's fine with me."

She rubbed her hands together while wondering what was going through his mind. There was an odd, speculative look on his face, as though he were thinking about her, the room, or both. Or maybe something far different.

"Well, since you find everything agreeable, I'd better get back to my cooking. Supper should be ready in thirty minutes. After we eat you can sign the lease."

"Sounds fine. Thank you, Claire."

She gave him another smile, then turned to leave. Sometime during their conversation the room had quit being a room and had become a bedroom. She'd been uncomfortably aware of the huge four-poster just a step away, and even more aware of the virile man standing beside her.

Shutting the door behind her, Claire took a moment to draw in a deep breath. For heaven's sake, what was the matter with her? So the man had nice eyes and broad shoulders. She'd been around nice-eyed men before. She'd even been married to one once, and that once had been enough. She was a mature woman now. She knew men and the working of their ways. She was far too old to let a man get under her skin.

Purposefully Claire hurried down the staircase and out to the kitchen. Madison McCrea was going to be here six or eight weeks. That was a long time, she told herself. After he'd been here a few days he would seem just like any other guest, just like any other man. She was sure of it.

Chapter Two

After Claire left the room, Madison shed his clothes and climbed into the shower. The day had been long, wet and muddy. There'd been trouble putting up a steel I beam and then a truck hauling in the heating and cooling systems had gotten stuck, burying nearly all of its eighteen wheels in the muddy work yard.

Madison hadn't had a peaceful moment to draw breath. But the past few moments with Claire had relaxed him and now he found himself humming as he lathered himself beneath the spray of water. He wondered if there was a man in Claire's life, and if there wasn't, why a woman like her would be alone.

You've come here to build a motel, he told himself, not woo a woman. Well, he hadn't gone so far as to plan wooing her. But there certainly wouldn't be any harm in getting to know her. After all, she was going to be his landlady.

Out of the shower, Madison pulled on a pair of jeans, a black sweatshirt and a clean pair of cowboy boots. The muddy ones he'd left behind on the front porch would have to be dealt with later.

At the bottom of the staircase, Madison followed his nose to the kitchen. He found Claire putting stuffed pork chops on a thick white platter.

"Smells good in here. Is there anything I can do?"

She looked up to see Madison striding into the kitchen, a warm smile on his face. For a moment her breath caught and her hand holding the spatula stopped midway to the dish on the countertop.

"No. It's kind of you to offer, but everything is ready." She dropped her gaze, feeling foolish. It didn't hurt to look at the man, she told herself. He was attractive; he wasn't poison.

"I can carry," he insisted.

She placed the last chop on the platter, then glanced up at him. He was hovering over her, big as life. The clean scent of soap and cologne emanated from him, telling Claire he'd been showering while she'd finished cooking the meal. His hair was still wet. He'd slicked it away from his forehead, but already some of the unruly waves were beginning to fall forward.

Claire drew in a steadying breath and handed him the platter. "I serve meals on the back porch. Liv is already out there. She'll show you where to put that."

He nodded and left with the dish. Claire hurriedly gathered coffee and iced tea onto a silver tray. When she reached the porch, Liv and Madison were already chatting it up like old friends.

Liv spoke in a scolding voice. "Claire, you didn't tell me our new houseguest was from Beaumont."

"I didn't?" she asked offhandedly while placing the tray on a side table. "Does that make a difference?"

"Of course! My mother was from Beaumont. We used to spend some wonderful times there. Madison even knows an old friend of mine who owns a car dealership there—Carl Casey," she reminisced. "Is he gray-headed now?" she asked Madison. "He used to have the most wonderful head of black hair."

Madison smiled indulgently at Liv. "I'm afraid he's been gray-headed ever since I've known him. He has five grandchildren, I think."

"Oh, how lovely," Liv said with a sigh. "My daughter was never able to bear children so my late husband and I missed out on the joy of having grandchildren."

"That's too bad," Madison told the older woman.

There was such a note of genuine sympathy in Madison's voice that Claire's eyes turned to him. He was pulling out Liv's chair for her, and it was obvious from the dreamy smile on the woman's face that she was already charmed by the man.

"The most favorite lady in my life was my grandmother. Anything I wanted to talk about she understood," Madison remarked.

"Is she still living?" Liv asked.

Madison shook his head. "No. She passed on three years ago. She was nearly ninety."

"Tea or coffee, Madison?" Claire asked him.

"Coffee, please. Where do I sit?"

"Here," Claire told him, motioning to a chair just opposite her and to Liv's left.

Claire placed the drinks on the table. Madison waited until she was seated before he seated himself.

Claire thought it extremely gracious of him and was a little surprised by his manners. She'd expected him to be one of those tough, macho, beer-drinking, feet-on-the-table kind of men. Obviously his "Mama," as he'd called her, had been a genteel woman. Which made Claire wonder even more about his background.

"How long have you been in the construction business, Madison?" Liv asked as Claire began to pass around the food.

"All in all, about twelve years. When I was eighteen I started working for a friend's father who owned a construction company. I liked it and decided I wanted to have one of my own some day."

Claire placed a chop on her plate and handed him the dish. "I'm sure it took more than just deciding to come up with your own construction company to actually do it," she said.

He took two of the chops and handed the plate to Liv, who was looking from Claire to Madison with an undisguised gleam in her eye.

"That it did, ma'am—er, Claire. I started out very small, and even then I had a hard time getting a bank to back me. They somehow have the notion that just because you're young, you're a bad risk. But after a lot of hard work, the note was paid and of course that led to bigger and better things."

Claire handed him a bowl of corn on the cob. "And how young were you? Surely not eighteen!"

Madison chuckled. "Not quite, but I might as well have been. I was twenty-two, just out of college with an engineering degree."

Claire wondered just how long ago that had been but she wasn't about to ask. His age shouldn't interest her.

Feeding him and making him comfortable was all her job as a hostess required.

"Well, I for one can't understand why someone would want to invest in another motel in Eureka Springs," Liv commented. "Land sakes, the place is full of them now."

Claire spooned a portion of snap beans on her plate. She'd been simmering them all afternoon with bacon bits. It was a favorite dish among the guests she'd had over the years. She wondered if Madison would appreciate it.

"This is a tourist town, Liv," Claire reminded the woman. "In the height of vacation season rooms are very scarce. You know that."

"Well, yes," Liv reluctantly agreed. "But how would it pay for itself in the wintertime? I'm sure it's costing a fortune to have it built, isn't it Madison?"

Madison nodded. "A small one. But the financier is a Texas oilman. He can easily afford it."

"You know him?" Liv asked eagerly.

Claire gave the woman a hopeless look. Liv had an insatiable curiosity. Sometimes she could become downright offensive with her personal questions. "Liv, Madison may not want to discuss such personal things!"

Madison waved his fork in a dismissive gesture. "It's all right, Claire. A lot of people are curious about Texas oilmen. I know—my daddy is one."

"Oh," Liv uttered in a completely fascinated way.

Claire's eyes drifted to his face. If his father had been a Texas oilman, why had he needed to worry about a business loan? she wondered.

Madison began to eat his pork chop. He looked over at Claire and smiled. "This is delicious. Do you cook breakfast this good, too?"

"Oh, mercy," Liv groaned. "Claire gets up at a god-forsaken hour and fixes all those heavy things like biscuits and gravy, hash browns, grits. Give me a bowl of cereal any day."

"Breakfast is my favorite meal of the day," Claire reasoned. "I like for it to be substantial."

"Now, isn't that fine. Because I love breakfast, too," Madison drawled. "Gets my motor started."

Liv laughed and winked at Madison. "That's two things you both already have in common."

Claire's face began to turn a flame-red color. She'd hoped Liv had gotten over playing cupid. Obviously she hadn't. Madison was the first male guest they'd had in a while and it looked as though Liv was going to make the most of it. She had to stifle a long, soulful sigh.

Madison glanced curiously at Liv. "Oh really? What's the other thing?" he asked Liv.

"Your voices," the older woman explained. "You both have the same accent. I suppose that's because Claire is originally from Baton Rouge. That's not far from Beaumont."

"Just a little hop east," Madison replied.

"Would you like something else?" Claire asked him before giving Liv a chance to come up with another remark. "Some steak sauce? More coffee?"

"Coffee would be nice."

Claire got up and retrieved the pot from the side table. As she leaned over Madison's shoulder to refill his cup, she gripped the handle tightly. There was something about this man that set her on edge and if her hands were shaking anything like her insides, the coffee would go sloshing all over his arm.

God help her, she was thirty-five years old. She hadn't reacted to a man like this in years. Not even Saul, who was considered quite a catch here in the area. She'd dated him several times, but his smooth looks had left her unaffected. Since her divorce some twelve years ago, she'd looked upon men as creatures to be taken lightly. And that was the way she wanted to take this one. Lightly. Very lightly. But her senses were telling her something entirely different.

While Claire was at it, she refilled Liv's tea glass and replenished her own coffee cup. She noticed that the rain was still falling, but since there was no wind, the screened-in porch was nice and dry.

"Do you have a wife, Madison?" Liv suddenly spoke.

Claire was returning to her seat and nearly tripped at Liv's forward question.

He smiled patiently at the older woman. "No. I never believed I'd be good at that sort of thing. Besides, I've only had three women propose to me and I'd be weak-willed to give in before the seventh or eight, don't you think?"

"Oh, Madison," Liv said with a knowing smile. "I'm sure you've had a flock of women wanting to marry you. You're a good-looking young man."

Claire kept her attention on her plate. Madison could deal with Liv's questions himself, she decided.

"Thank you, Liv. But I'm afraid you have it all wrong. There're not too many women out on a construction site."

"Well," Liv replied as she cut into her chop, "if I were only thirty years younger I'd give you a chase."

"Liv!" Claire gasped.

Madison laughed and Liv laughed along with him.

"Claire, Madison knows I'm only teasing. You're so stuffy sometimes." The older woman looked at Madison with a pointed expression. "Do you know Claire was dating a very handsome man here in town, but she dropped him because he kissed her behind the ear? I thought, my Lord, Claire, are you crazy? I'd give my ear away if I could have my Frank back."

"Liv! How can you talk this way in front of Madison? You don't even know him, and he certainly doesn't want to hear this nonsense!" She gave the older woman a cutting glare, hoping she would get the message once and for all. "Besides," she added defensively, "the ear had nothing to do with my dropping him. He was a boor."

Liv waved her hand back and forth. "Of course I know Madison. He's a nice young man from Beaumont who owns a construction business and his daddy is in oil. He's currently building a motel. He's good-looking and single, but he doesn't have time for women. Isn't that right, Madison?"

If Claire had been able to look at him, she would have seen he was on the verge of bursting with laughter.

"Oh, yeah, that's right. Of course, that last part could change. I mean, if there was a woman around who caught my interest, I could always make extra time for her."

Liv reached over and patted his hand. "I knew you were my kind of man."

Madison grinned as he helped himself to more beans. "I was always good at communicating with women. Maybe I have my mother and grandmother to thank for that. Southern women are sensitive, you know. If a man can understand a Southern woman, he can understand any of them."

Claire began to choke and hurriedly reached for her coffee. At the same moment the front doorbell rang. Liv jumped up to go answer it.

"I'll get it," she called. "It's probably Grace wanting me to go to bingo with her."

Thank God, Claire thought as the scalding coffee slid down her throat.

"Are you okay?" Madison asked, noting the moisture in her eyes. She had damn beautiful eyes, he thought. They'd struck him the moment he'd seen her and now that he was closer, he could see they were hazel. A dark mixture of green and gold.

"Yes, I'm fine now." She set her cup back on its saucer and reached for her fork. She'd barely touched any of her food, and now she pushed at the snap beans with very little appetite.

"I'm sorry if Liv embarrassed you," she went on, not really knowing what to say. "She's very outspoken. But actually she's a dear. She misses her late husband terribly and sometimes she...overcompensates."

"It would take a lot more than a dear little gray-haired lady to embarrass me."

She lifted her head and as their eyes clashed she had the feeling that he really did understand women. Maybe a bit too much, she thought.

"Yes," she said softly, "I think perhaps it would."

As they continued to look at each other the smile fell from Madison's face. He tried to remember back to other times and other women. Had it felt this way when he'd looked at them? He didn't think so. There was something in her eyes, on her face, that touched him in some unknown place he hadn't even known he had. Careful, Madison, he told himself, she's not the love 'em and leave 'em type. And that's the only type you can manage in your life.

Clearing his throat, he pulled his attention back to his plate and reached for his coffee cup. "This is beautiful country up here in Arkansas. I hadn't seen this area until about a month ago. How long have you lived here?"

Claire forced herself to eat and relax. "Five years. My aunt owned this house and when she died she left it to me. Up until then I was still living in Baton Rouge."

"So you've lived here five years," he mused aloud. "I take it that means you like it here?"

Without looking his way, Claire shrugged. "Well, I saw an opportunity with the house. And there wasn't anything tying me down to Baton Rouge."

Madison was mulling over Claire's statement when he heard raised voices coming from the house.

Claire turned her head toward the doorway. "That must be Arthur. He's Liv's beau, or maybe I should say, on the days Liv lets him be."

Moments later the older woman appeared in the doorway. "Goodbye, you two. I'm leaving with Arthur."

Claire gave her a dry look. "I thought he was a lothario and that you didn't even want to think of the man."

"Now, Claire," she pouted, "don't you be difficult. He brought chocolates. What's a woman to do?"

"You could try saying no," Claire suggested.

"Well, that wouldn't be any fun at all. Would it, Madison?"

Madison laughed softly as he looked at both women. "I never did like the word no myself."

"You see," she told Claire with a smug smile. "Madison agrees."

Sighing, Claire turned back to her dinner. "I'll leave the downstairs door unlocked for you," she said, knowing Liv had already decided to go with Arthur the minute she opened the door.

Liv hurried away. By now Claire had totally lost interest in the food on her plate.

"I wonder what her late husband was like?" Madison said.

Putting her fork aside and leaning back in her chair, Claire said. "Very tired, I imagine."

Madison's laughter burst out, filling the room with the unexpected sound. Claire found herself smiling at him. She couldn't help it. There was a warmth about him that drew a person in.

"So you have a humorous side to you," he said, still chuckling.

"Well, some people might say I have to work at it."

Madison shook his head. "I doubt that."

He wished she would keep on smiling. It made her face glow, and her teeth were so white and sexy against her red lips.

Claire pushed back her chair and got to her feet. "Now that you're nearly through with this hectic meal, would you like dessert? It's lemon pie."

His gaze went down the length of her curvy body as though he wished he could have a taste of her for dessert instead of the pie. Claire felt a rush of heat swamp her.

"Sounds nice. Thank you."

Damn it, Claire, she scolded herself as she headed back to the kitchen. Men look at you every day. There's nothing different about the way this one is looking at you. But there was, another voice inside her spoke up. When his eyes were on her, she felt naked and shaky and crazy. She felt like a woman, and that wasn't good. That wasn't good at all.

Quickly she sliced the pie, deciding that this situation would never work. She would just have to tell him that she couldn't offer him the room. She could use the excuse that she'd forgotten someone had reserved it for next week.

Claire had just put the pieces of pie on serving plates when the telephone rang. Taking down the phone from the wall, she spoke into the receiver. A man's voice was on the end of the line requesting to speak to Madison.

"Just a minute, please," she told the caller and hurried out to get him. "You have a telephone call. You can take it in the living room or your room upstairs."

Madison rose from the table and tossed down his napkin. "Thank you, I'll take it in my room. Oh, and could you save that pie for me?" he added with a grin for her.

She stepped back as he brushed by her. "Surely," she murmured, then watched with a bit of relief as he disappeared down the hallway.

Madison's call wasn't a short one. After five minutes Claire decided to clear away the mess from the table. After fifteen minutes she had most of the dishes washed and was trying to decide on the best way to let him know he couldn't stay here.

She was taking the cowardly way out, she knew. But this time it couldn't be helped. Madison McCrea was a dangerous man. She couldn't allow him to come into her home and disrupt her life. And that was what would happen. She could feel it in her bones.

More than thirty minutes later, Claire was putting away the dried dishes when Madison strode into the kitchen.

"Sorry. The call took much longer than I thought. I hope you didn't throw away that pie."

Taking a deep breath, she turned and looked at him. The moment she met his blue eyes she felt her earlier resolve crumbling. Claire hated herself for the weakness.

"No, it's here on the kitchen table. But if you'd prefer you can take it out to the back porch."

"No, this is fine. As long as you'll join me."

He sat down on the bench and slid his long legs beneath the table. Claire knew the only gracious thing for a hostess to do was get forks and coffee and join him.

Once they were both eating the lemon meringue, she asked in a casual voice, "Are you sure you still want to stay here? After meeting Liv and all?"

"Liv won't bother me. I'll only be here at night. And something tells me that Liv is usually gone with Arthur anyway. Am I right?"

Claire nodded, realizing he had her on that point. "Usually. But you're a good distance from your job site. You could possibly find a room closer to your work."

He gave her a puzzled look. "Are you trying to get rid of me?"

She felt her cheeks turn pink at his question. "Uh...no. I just want to make sure you're completely satisfied here before you sign the lease."

Madison swallowed a bite of pie. "Why don't you go get it now? I'll sign it and we can get this issue out of the way."

Apparently he intended to stay and Claire couldn't bring herself to be crass enough to tell him he had to make other arrangements. Besides, she quickly reminded herself, she rented rooms to make a living and Madison was a paying customer. It was the only way she could look at it.

"I'll be right back," she assured him. "Feel free to use anything in the kitchen you'd like." Except me, she added silently.

When she returned, he was helping himself to another cup of coffee. For a moment Claire allowed her eyes to drift down the length of him. He was a tall man with long, muscular legs. The width of his muscular shoulders and the narrowness of his waist made Claire wonder if he worked out with weights, but she somehow doubted it. The man obviously didn't have time for it. She'd rather think he was a natural. In more ways than one.

"I hope you don't mind me helping myself," he spoke as he took his seat at the table. "You don't know what this means to me. Finding a place like this where I can really relax. This is almost like being home."

Claire warmed to his words. While in her early teens, she lost her parents and what little home life she'd had. Maybe that was why she liked making her guests feel at home. Because she knew what it was like not to have one. "You like being home?"

He nodded. "But I also like my job and sometimes the two are separated. Up until now I've stayed in motel rooms when I've been away on the job. That kind of life really gets a person old quick."

Claire knew she'd feel the same way if she were in his shoes. "Here's the lease," she said, handing him the single sheet of paper. "Just fill out the simple bit of information at the top, then sign at the bottom. If you'd rather, you can pay later."

He took the pen she offered him and began to scribble boldly across the empty lines. "I'd like to pay you now. For six weeks at least. After that I'll just have to wait and see how things go."

Six weeks! How could she be in this man's company for six weeks? Yet it was too late to be worrying about that question. "If that's the way you want it."

After completing the form he pulled out a worn leather billfold from his back pocket, and without batting an eye he counted out the bills. She folded the money and pushed it into her jeans pocket. Somehow she felt strange about taking his money. He wasn't like other guests, damn his blue eyes.

"Thank you," she murmured.

"I'm the one who should be saying thank you," he said, stretching his long legs out in front of him and taking a sip of his coffee. "And I do, I want you to know that."

She moved away from him and poured herself a cup of coffee just to have something to do. "Have you met anyone since you've come to Eureka Springs?"

"Just the men down at the lumberyard."

"Well, I suppose your men are all from Beaumont," she commented.

"Yes," he replied. "Most of them are friends and have worked for me for several years."

"You probably like to go out with them in the evenings. Drink beer, shoot pool."

"Not really," he said, his eyes on her. She was standing at the kitchen counter, staring out the window over the sink. Her figure was lush and full. Every time he looked at her his breath caught, his heart pounded, and he felt unusually young and foolish. "I usually have paperwork to deal with, and I see enough of the men on the site. Besides, I never was much of a pool player."

Claire wondered what he did like to play at. It was hard for her to believe he lived such a single-minded life. Work and nothing more. He was too young, too attractive and too downright virile to be without a woman for too long. He wasn't fooling her!

"What do you do in the evenings?" he asked. "Especially now that you've dropped the boor who kissed you behind the ear?"

Claire felt hot color rush to her cheeks. "I wish to heaven that Liv could keep her mouth shut. It wasn't really like that at all."

She heard him shifting on the bench and turned her head to see he'd gotten up from the table and was walking toward her.

"Oh? Then he didn't kiss you behind the ear?"

Claire toyed nervously with her dark hair. "Yes, he did, but—" Her lips compressed in a thin line as she watched a cocky grin spread across his face. "I have plenty to keep me busy in the evenings."

"I'll bet. Like doing the dishes and not getting kissed."

He was standing over her now, so near that a fold in his sweatshirt was almost touching her breast. She felt herself quaking inside and she swallowed nervously. She knew how to deal with men; she'd been close to them before. But not this one. He was doing strange things to her mind and body.

"Something like that," she murmured, not letting herself look up at him.

His right hand came up and suddenly Claire felt his finger touch the soft skin behind her ear.

"Sounds like a slow life."

Her eyes came up to his. His touch compelled them to.

"I like things slow."

"Isn't that something? So do I," he said huskily, dropping his hand away from her.

Claire's nostrils flared with indignation. "But I don't like presumptuous men."

Madison's thick dark brows lifted innocently. "Presumptuous? Me? My goodness, you are a touchy woman."

Claire folded her arms over her breast in a protective gesture. "No, Mr. McCrea, I'm not "touchy" at all. And I can already see that this situation just isn't going to work."

He chuckled, his expression one of disbelief. "Whoa now, I didn't know there was a situation."

Claire wondered why, at a time like this, she should be thinking how good his voice sounded. She should have been thinking of a way to put him in his place. Yet all she could manage to do was glare at him.

"I believe Liv was telling the truth about you," he said, his voice losing some of its humor. "You probably did drop that guy for kissing you. Because I can see all over your face that you'd like to boot me out of here, too."

"Would you like to go?" she offered none too sweetly.

"I'm not about to."

"Then let's get one thing straight. I'm your landlady," she said coolly, her chin lifting a fraction.

He gave her another cocky grin as he set his coffee cup down in the sink behind her. He had to lean over her to reach it and his arm brushed her shoulder in the process. "I know. Thanks for the pie."

With that, he turned and left the room. Claire watched him, not knowing whether to curse a blue streak or burst into tears. She'd suspected him before of being trouble. Now she definitely knew he was.

Chapter Three

It was a long time before Claire left the kitchen. She swept the floor, then swept it again, then told herself she was acting like an idiot.

She couldn't ignore the man forever. Besides, he was probably up in his room and wouldn't come down till morning. She certainly hoped so. That would give her time to put everything in its right perspective. Maybe in the morning she could see that she'd overreacted. After all, he'd barely touched her on the side of the neck. It wasn't as though he'd made an advance or propositioned her.

The dark living room was empty. After switching on a table lamp, Claire looked out the windows and saw that the rain was still falling steadily. She would love to take a long walk and forget about Madison McCrea, but a walk was out of the question. She'd be soaked in a matter of moments.

Wandering around the room, picking up objects and putting them back down, Claire finally turned on the television. However, after a few minutes she realized none of the programs could hold her attention so she turned it off.

Frustrated, she sat down on the couch and grabbed a magazine. It was full of ads with sleek-looking models. Their faces and bodies were young and smooth with most of them presenting a sexy image.

Claire couldn't remember a time when she'd wanted to look sexy. Perhaps, long ago she had. When she'd been very young she'd played the part that men seemed to want women to play. But after she and Larry had divorced, disillusionment had set in. She'd tried so hard to be the perfect wife for him. Just as her mother had tried to be the perfect wife for her father. But it hadn't worked on either count. She'd come away from the experiences feeling like a hard empty shell, and in all these years that feeling had never left her.

Footsteps on the staircase had her automatically closing the magazine and turning her head toward the sound. Madison was stepping off the bottom step. He saw her almost instantly and gave a smile as though nothing was amiss between them. Which Claire supposed was so. There wasn't anything between them, she assured herself.

"I have to go out," he said as he strode toward the door.

"Oh." The one word was all she could come up with. What did he expect? For her to question his comings and goings?

His hand resting on the doorknob, he glanced over his shoulder at her. "You wouldn't happen to know where a good laundry is, would you?"

"I'm afraid all the full-service laundries are closed now. It's nearly eight."

Frowning, he said, "I guess I'll have to settle for one where you put in the coins and do it yourself."

"I think there's one of those on the west side of town. I'm not sure."

There was a blue cap on his head that had the words McCrea Construction on the front. He reached up and tugged the bill a fraction lower on his forehead.

"You wouldn't want to come along and show me where it is, would you? I'm going to have to go to work naked tomorrow if I don't get some clean jeans."

His laundry was not her problem. "Please spare our city," she said, looking back at her magazine with pointed interest.

"To be honest, I don't know anything about doing laundry."

"Few men do."

"What do you expect, Claire? I can't be good at everything."

His cocky sense of humor was so outrageous she couldn't remain aloof with him. With a compliant smile, she rose from the couch. "Bring them downstairs. I'll do them for you."

"Oh no! A deal is a deal. You do the linen, that's all. If you could just give me a rundown on what to do, I'll try it."

"First you have to separate the clothes."

He grinned at her and Claire felt that unreasonable racing of her heart start all over again.

"Right. In little piles on the floor. I used to see my Mama do that. I just never knew what the piles were for."

Claire stifled a groan. "You have to put similar fabrics together. In other words, you can't wash your underwear with your jeans."

"I can't? Damn, I would have done that right off. See, you really need to go with me."

She really didn't need to go with him, she thought desperately. "I offered to do them for you," she reasoned.

"No, that would be going against the deal. Besides, it's a lovely night. You need to get out."

A lovely night? It was pouring. She'd have to ride with him in his pickup. They'd be confined together in that small little space and she'd have to look over at him. She'd be able to smell his cologne, and he'd probably give her two or three more of those grins of his. By then she'd be thinking things she hadn't thought of in years.

"Claire? Did you hear me? I said I'd really appreciate your help. Maybe I can do something in return for you. I'm a good carpenter."

She focused her mind back on his words. "I thought you were an engineer."

"I am. But I can bring myself down to using a hammer and nails. Whatever the situation requires."

She didn't doubt his abilities as a carpenter. But she still wasn't keen on the idea of being alone in his company. Still, she would feel terrible if he ruined all his clothes. Especially when he'd asked so nicely for her help.

"I suppose I could go with you this once and show you what to do."

"I'd be eternally in your debt," he drawled, his warm eyes following her as she moved across the room.

Something about his voice told her he'd probably had lots of success in talking women into his way of thinking. The idea that she was another on the list didn't make her feel one bit better.

Heading for the closet, she said, "Let me get a jacket and I'll be ready."

It was still raining when they walked to Madison's truck. Claire pulled the hood of her coat over her head so her hair wouldn't be soaked.

Inside the pickup she quickly looked around for a space large enough to sit on. All sorts of papers were scattered across the seat. Some looked like blueprints, others shipping orders and invoices. A yellow hard hat was resting on the gearshift on the floor, while a toolbox and a pair of black cowboy boots filled the area beneath her feet.

Madison quickly moved some of the things. "Here, let me get that out of your way. I guess you can tell I haven't had much time for cleaning."

Claire eased down on the seat and pushed the hood of her jacket off her dark hair. "There's no need to apologize. I'm sure you're a busy man."

She propped her feet on the toolbox as he started the engine. When the dash lights came on she noticed the top of it was lined with paper cups, some of them still half-filled with cold coffee. Alongside the cups were two sets of leather gloves, a pair of wire-framed sunglasses and a black rubber snake.

"I take it the snake has some meaning in all of this?" she asked.

Madison laughed as he shifted the truck into motion. "Some of the boys thought it would be amusing to put it in the foreman's lunch pail. That snake caused a few black eyes and loose teeth."

"Did you fire the men?"

He looked at her as though he found her question surprising. "No. The men were only having a little fun. They just didn't realize Ray would get so riled to find a snake among his bologna sandwiches." He shrugged as though this wasn't the first escapade with his men that he'd had to deal with. "So I took the snake and the boys are buying Ray's lunch for two weeks."

So he was diplomatic along with charming, she reluctantly admitted. "Do you have a family other than your oilman daddy?"

His eyes returned to the road ahead of them. "Dad, Mama and a brother one year older than me."

"How old are you?" The question came out of Claire before she could stop it. She was glad the interior of the pickup was dark because she knew her face was livid red.

"Thirty-one," he answered. "Why? How old are you?"

Claire gasped. "That's none of your business."

He laughed easily. "My age was none of your business. But I told you anyway."

Groaning inwardly, she mumbled, "Thirty-five."

He didn't say anything and she hoped that now he knew her age he would look at her in a different light and lay those bedroom eyes of his on some other unsuspecting female.

"You said that like someone had a noose around your neck. Don't you like your age?" he asked.

His question took her by surprise. "Like it?" she repeated, her eyes studying him as he drove through the rain and darkness. The streets of Eureka Springs were steep and winding. She was glad because it forced him to keep his attention on his driving. "Does anyone ever like their age? I thought every adult wanted to be younger and every child wanted to be older."

"I don't want to be younger," he said. "I like the age I am, and so should you. Why would you want to be younger?"

She thought about his question for a moment. "I've never really asked myself that question before. But I do know it would rid me of a few sags and wrinkles. That would be nice."

His smile said he found her words amusing. "I didn't see any sags or wrinkles, and believe me I'm a good judge. Besides, you don't seem that vain to me."

She wasn't vain and she was glad he'd noticed that about her. Although it was disconcerting to know he'd looked at her that closely.

"I'm not. But a woman likes to look her best."

He geared down and braked at a red light. Looking over at her, he smiled as if he enjoyed having her just an arm's length away. "Why do you women worry so much about your looks?"

Claire crossed her legs and tried to settle herself more comfortably. Yet the casual position was deceptive. Every nerve in her body was standing at attention, focusing on him.

"Probably because since time began men have made it known that they covet a woman's beauty."

"You think so?" he asked in a surprised voice. "Personally I like women for their minds. They're never predictable, therefore never boring."

Claire wondered how they'd ever gotten into such a philosophical conversation. "Well, my ex-husband liked women for their looks," she said tightly.

So she'd been married, Madison concluded. He wanted to ask her about it. But this was hardly the time. He'd known her only a day. He didn't want to put her on guard with such a personal question.

The traffic light turned green and Claire instructed him to turn right. After traveling about three blocks, they found a Laundromat on the corner. It was open for business, but there wasn't anyone inside. Claire figured there wasn't anyone else crazy enough to carry out their laundry on a night like this.

Madison's clothes were in two weatherproof bags in the back of the truck. He carried them in while Claire looked around the room for a change machine. Once they'd turned several bills into quarters, Claire began to help him sort the clothes.

"Jeans in one pile, underwear in one pile and shirts in another, right?" he asked.

Claire looked up as she stuffed a pair of jeans down into one of the washers to see Madison holding up a white shirt. "Well, it's not that cut and dried," she said. "That will go into the underwear pile because it's white."

"Well damn. Some of my underwear isn't white. Does that mean it'll go into the shirt pile?"

The confusion on his face had Claire suddenly laughing. "That's what it means."

"See, I told you this would be too confusing for a man like me."

Claire took the shirt from him and tossed it in with the rest of the white things. "And I'm a real savior for coming with you," she said.

"An angel," he assured her. "A real angel."

Claire gave him a dry look because she knew he would have said the same thing to any woman.

In a matter of moments they had the clothes loaded into the washing machines. Claire put the quarters into the slots and Madison pushed in the levers to get them started.

After the clothes were swishing in sudsy water the two of them found a couple of chairs and sat down by the windows overlooking the rain-slick street.

Madison said, "Why are we the only ones in here?"

"Probably because no one else worries about getting out and doing their laundry at nine o'clock at night in a blinding rain."

Madison chuckled. "Are you always this testy?"

Claire had to smile at him because she knew she hadn't been testy with him and he was only teasing her. "No. I'm not always this gullible, either."

To be honest, Claire had never gone anywhere with any of her guests before. She did her best to make them comfortable in her home, but as far as getting personal with any of them, she never had. Except Liv. But Liv was different. Liv got personal with everyone she came in contact with. Obviously Madison was different, too, because here she was breaking a rule she'd always put upon herself.

Madison lifted the blue cap from his head and ran his fingers through his hair. "That boor," he began as he settled the cap back on his head and rested his eyes on her face, "did he ever tell you how pretty you are?"

She wasn't ready for his words and her mouth fell open.

"Maybe. I don't remember," she said, finally collecting herself enough to speak.

He gave her a pointed smile that had Claire shifting uncomfortably in her seat.

"Saul was more interested in his own looks than he was in mine," she explained. "And since you keep insisting on pestering me with your questions, how many women go around telling you how attractive you are?"

Laughing, he stretched his longs legs out in front of him and crossed his boots at the ankles. "Hoards of them. Why, just today I had to let this cap out another inch. Swelled head. It does that to me."

His nonsense had her tossing him a dry look. "I don't believe for a minute that you're too busy for the opposite sex. I'll bet you left a fiancée back home just pining for your return."

Madison stared at her in horror. In the background the washers all began to make a clanging noise as they shifted into spin cycle. "Don't attach that word to me! I get a heart attack just hearing about it."

"Which word? Woman or fiancée?"

"The last. I'm not a marrying man. Leastwise, not for the next ten, maybe twenty years."

A smug look came over Claire's face. "Isn't that a coincidence? I'm not a marrying woman."

Madison's eyes couldn't help themselves. They drifted up and down her legs encased in the tight blue jeans, across her slender waist, then up to her full breasts. He'd noticed more than once that they jiggled when she moved a certain way, sending his temperature up a notch.

So she wasn't the marrying kind, he silently considered. Maybe she was the just-have-an-affair kind. But Madison really doubted it. She'd thrown a fit just because he'd touched her behind the ear. He couldn't see her having wild wanton sex with a man. He couldn't see her having sex at all, unless the man was him. The idea was so surprising to Madison that the color actually drained from his face.

Claire noticed the pallor on his cheeks and wondered if he was coming down with something. "Are you tired? You look a little pale."

He pulled his legs up and folded his arms across his chest. "It was that word you used. Scares me to death," he said in a joking voice.

Claire studied him closer. The hooded expression in his face contradicted his voice, making her wonder what the man was really thinking. She'd already decided she'd never met anyone like him before, and she wondered just what else she would discover about the man before his six weeks' stay was over.

"Have you ever been married? Engaged?"

Madison grimaced. "That's all I've heard out of my parents for the past five years. 'You need a wife, Madison.' But I haven't yet figured out for what."

Claire really didn't know, either. With his looks he probably had all the women he wanted anyway. Why would he want to tie himself down to just one? All the men in Claire's life hadn't been able to handle committing themselves to only one woman. It would be crazy to think this man was any different.

"I know what you mean," Claire said pointedly. "Liv keeps telling me I need a man. But I haven't figured what I need one for, either."

Beneath lowered lids, Madison's eyes slid down her smooth throat and along the V of her shirt. He could think of a million and one ways to make her need him, and not one of them was carrying out the garbage. Just the idea of having her ripe body next to his caused a strange curling sensation in the pit of his stomach.

"Is your brother married?" Claire asked, completely unaware of the thoughts running through Madison's head.

His mouth slanted with a mockery that took Claire by surprise. "Oh yes," he said dryly. "He's the perfect husband. The perfect father."

"Is there something wrong with that?" she asked.

"No. It's just that those things are for Mitch. Not for me."

"Is he in the construction business, too?"

Madison laughed shortly. "Mitch wouldn't be caught dead in the construction business. He's a wildcatter."

"Oh, an oilman like your dad. I see," Claire said. But actually she didn't. She was picking up signals from his voice that told her all was not right between him and his brother. She wondered if there'd been a rift or rivalry over a woman, but she didn't intend to ask. That was too personal a question, and it was really none of her business, she reminded herself.

"Yeah, like my dad," he repeated softly.

His eyes trailed over to the windows and the passing traffic. Claire could feel him turn inside himself, as though speaking of his family had turned his mind to far different things.

She respected his privacy and sat there quietly examining her own feelings. In the past hour she'd learned something about Madison McCrea. She'd learned that she liked him. Whether that was good or bad she didn't know yet.

It was only a matter of a few minutes before the washers shut off. Claire went over to the machines and lifted the lids. Madison was close on her heels.

"What do we do now?" he asked.

"Now we put them in the dryers," she told him.

He helped her unload the clothes into a rolling basket, then pushed it to the opposite side of the room where the wall was lined with dryers.

"Surely there's not any trick to this," he said. "Don't you just toss the clothes in and turn on the machines?"

Claire had to laugh. She hadn't realized he would be as lost in a Laundromat as she would be on a construction site.

"Well, there's a little more than that to it. You still have to keep things separated, because different types of fabric need to be dried at different temperatures."

He shook his head. "I should have known."

They put enough money in the machines to keep them running for thirty minutes. However, after that length of time the jeans were still damp, so Madison dropped in more quarters.

While they waited for the jeans to finish, Claire demonstrated to Madison how to smooth and fold the already dried clothes. He tried his hand at folding a few T-shirts, but they looked sloppy compared to Claire's.

She said, "Don't feel badly. I could never read a blueprint. Besides, doing laundry isn't that meaningful."

Madison folded a handkerchief and placed it on a pile. It was one piece of laundry he could manage. "It's very meaningful to me," he told Claire. "I hate wearing dirty clothes, and I think you're right—this town isn't ready to see me naked."

Claire didn't look at him. She was afraid if she did, her eyes would start undressing him and he would see it and know she was attracted to him.

It was something Claire might as well admit to herself. She was attracted to Madison McCrea. A man younger than herself. A man who thought of women as just something to be enjoyed from time to time.

During the drive back to Claire's house, the rain eased somewhat. But it was still wet and sloppy out. After Madison parked the pickup and turned off the motor, she pulled on her hood before leaving the truck.

"I left the door unlocked," she told him. "So we wouldn't have to fumble with a key in the rain."

There was no light in Liv's upstairs window, telling Claire that the widow hadn't yet returned from playing bingo. It gave her a strange feeling to know that she and Madison would be in the house alone together. She didn't really understand why she should be having the feeling. She'd been alone with other male guests before. But none of them had looked or acted like Madison.

He carried both the cases filled with his clean clothes, even though Claire offered to carry one. Once in the house she led the way up the staircase and opened his door for him.

"Thanks," he said, entering the room behind her.

Claire went to the closet and opened it. "There should be plenty of clothes hangers here for you. If not, I can scrounge up some from my own closet."

"Don't worry about it. I doubt I'll hang up anything tonight anyway."

She turned and faced him. "I'd be happy to do that for you tomorrow. I'll have plenty of time throughout the day."

After Claire had made the offer, the idea suddenly came to her that he might not want her going through his things while he wasn't around. She hoped he didn't take her offer as an opportunity for her to snoop.

"That's very nice of you, Claire. Thanks. I'll dance at your wedding with cowbells on."

Starting toward the door, she smiled wanly at the old saying. "I'm afraid you'll have to repay me some other way because I'm sure I won't be attending anymore weddings unless it's that of a friend. Good night, Madison."

Realizing he didn't want to lose her company, he followed her to the door. "Good night, Claire. And thank you for everything."

Out in the hallway she turned around to face his tall form in the doorway. She smiled up at him, unaware that the look on her face was quietly provocative.

"It was nothing. And . . . and I'm sorry I reacted so strongly earlier down in the kitchen. I guess I'm just not used to being touched." Now that she'd had time to look at the whole incident, she knew it had meant nothing to Madison. He was the teasing sort and that was all that had been behind his actions.

Madison wondered if she realized how much of herself she was giving away with her admission. But she couldn't have said anything that would have pleased him more. Apparently she didn't have lovers, and if she had, it had been a long time ago. Sometime during supper and now Madison had accepted the fact that he wanted her. He intended to have her, too. Every sweet inch of her.

"Consider it forgotten," he assured her. "I have."

She let out a relieved sigh. "Good."

He watched her turn and go to her own room, then called a good-night to her again before she shut the door behind her.

You must be slipping, Madison, he told himself as he shut the bedroom door behind him. Before, you would have found some excuse to get her into your arms and into your bed.

But Claire was different, he told himself while shedding his black sweatshirt. He already knew that making love to her would be special. He didn't want to rush it. Once he had her, he wanted to savor every moment.

A knock at the door shattered his erotic thoughts. Tossing the sweatshirt aside, he went to answer it.

"I'm sorry to disturb you," she said to him.

Claire's eyes were on his face but somehow she could still see his massive chest. And that was the only word she could think of to describe it. The muscles were matted thickly with dark hair and beckoned her hands to reach up and touch. Instead, she gripped them together behind her back.

"You didn't disturb me. Is there a problem?"

Claire swallowed because her throat had suddenly become dry, her palms sweaty. "No. No problem. I was just wondering what time you'd like breakfast. I usually eat around six-thirty."

"That's perfect."

"I'll see you in the morning then," she told him.

"In the morning," he echoed.

His eyes filled with warmth as they traveled over her face, one corner of his mouth lifted into a little grin. Claire found herself smiling back at him before she stepped away from his door and returned to her room.

Chapter Four

Claire was an early riser. She always had been. She loved the morning hours when the sun had not yet appeared. Especially in the summer when the grass and flowers were covered with heavy dew and the birds were already singing in the trees.

She hummed along with the radio as she worked in the kitchen, telling herself she was in a lighthearted mood because the rain had stopped and the sky was clearing. After peeping in the oven to see if the biscuits were done, she spooned rich smelling coffee into the coffeemaker, then went to work placing several strips of bacon in a frying pan.

The coffee had dripped and she was placing the bacon on a paper towel to drain when Madison appeared in the kitchen. He was dressed in jeans again, which didn't surprise Claire because they were the only kind of pants she'd seen in his laundry last night. This morning he was wearing a white shirt with a tiny blue windowpane check running through it.

He walked toward her and Claire noticed the check matched the color of his eyes. She wondered if he'd worn the shirt on purpose because he knew how attractive he looked in it.

"Good morning," he said cheerfully. "It smells delicious in here."

"Thank you. I hope you're hungry."

"I'm ravenous."

He stood watching her stir milk into a frying pan filled with meat drippings. She was wearing a full pink skirt with a tiny print and a close-fitting top of matching pink with spaghetti straps that showed off her shoulders. They were beautiful shoulders, he thought. Not too small or bony. Not too heavy or muscled. They were the kind of shoulders a man liked to take hold of and draw the woman he wanted into his arms.

"Did you sleep well?" she asked.

Actually he hadn't. Not because the bed was uncomfortable, but because he'd kept imagining Claire in it beside him. "As well as can be expected when I'm in a strange bed."

Claire nodded as though she understood. "You'll get settled in after a few days. If you'd like to go ahead and pour the coffee, be my guest. Everything is almost ready here."

"Sure," he said, looking around for the pot. It was at the end of the cabinet. He carried the glass carafe to the table and filled the two cups already sitting on the bright red placemats.

There was a clay pot with a blooming African violet in the middle of the table. Closer to their plates and silverware were salt and pepper shakers, a saucer with butter on it that looked like the real thing, along with a jar of homemade jam.

"Do you take cream with your coffee?" she asked. She'd been too flustered last night at supper to remember.

"No. Just black." He returned the carafe to its hot plate.

"Do you like biscuits?"

"Love them," he answered.

"How about gravy and cottage fries?"

"Love them, too. Liv wasn't kidding. You really do cook breakfast, don't you?"

She smiled to herself as she pulled the buttermilk biscuits from the oven. "I really do."

He stepped back as she carried the hot pan to the table.

"Please, go ahead and sit down," she told him. "I won't mind if you start before me."

Madison sat down and took a sip of his coffee. It had the distinct flavor of Louisiana coffee, a mixture that he couldn't quite identify but remembered drinking on his visits to New Orleans. He supposed she'd picked up the taste for it while living in Baton Rouge.

"Liv doesn't come down for breakfast?" he asked.

Claire laughed softly as she joined him at the table. "Liv probably won't be down until ten. She's a late riser."

"You didn't really have to cook all this for me."

She smiled and shook her head. "I didn't. Besides, I'm used to cooking for guests. It's a part of the job."

Her words knocked the wind out of him. He reached for a biscuit, split it open and stuffed it with butter. Did she often cook like this for other men? Of course she did, he impatiently answered himself. The woman runs a boarding house. There'd probably been lots of men sitting in the same place he was sitting now.

Claire placed a spoonful of potatoes on her plate, then passed the dish to Madison. It was nice having someone to share breakfast with, she thought. Usually she was sitting here alone, with the radio her only companion.

"Actually I've never had a workingman for a boarder," she admitted. "Mostly I have couples, tourists who are traveling through the area."

Madison looked at her as he forked the potatoes to his mouth. Maybe his assumption had been wrong. He hoped so. It gave him a good feeling to think she'd never shared a breakfast like this with another man. Or at least not since her ex-husband.

"This is a beautiful part of the country. And cooler in the summer, I suppose, since you're in the mountains. I can see why you attract as many tourists as you do."

"It gets hot, but not like down on the flats. Our winters are pretty hard, though. We have heavy snows at times."

"I rarely ever see snow," he said. "Every Christmas I tell myself I'm going to go north where there's snow and spruce trees. But each year I end up going to the beach." He poured white gravy over a biscuit half, then took a bite. After he swallowed he said, "Where'd you learn to make gravy like this?"

His compliment pleased her. "My mother. She was a wonderful cook."

"You must have learned at an early age. I remember you saying they were killed when you were a teenager."

Regret crossed her face. "Yes, they were. But she had me in the kitchen when I was young. That was back in the time when most women's jobs were only that of mother and housekeeper. She spent lots of time with me, teaching me how to do the things a woman is supposed to know." Claire smiled wryly. "Mother would have been out of sync with the nineties."

Madison sipped his coffee slowly while trying to imagine Claire losing her parents at such a young age. He couldn't imagine growing up without his, even though he and his father had never really seen eye to eye on many things.

"What about your father? What did he do?" Madison asked.

Claire reached for a biscuit. "He was a welder. But mostly he was an alcoholic. That's what killed them, you see. He'd been drinking and driving. He did that quite often. But Mother always went with him anyway. She was so in love with him that it never occurred to her to go against his wishes."

"That's too bad." Madison didn't know what else to say. Obviously it had been a tragic period in her young life. He wondered how much it still affected her. He was sure it did. There was a quiver in her voice, a tinge of pain on her face that was too obvious to miss.

"Yes," Claire said quietly. "It was very bad."

"They left you all alone," he added. "You must have felt very bitter about that."

She looked at him with surprise, wondering how he'd been able to guess how she'd felt at the time. "Yes, I did.'' Then she smiled warmly. ''But that's enough about such depressing things. Tell me about some of the things you've built.''

He did, and Claire listened with pointed interest. By the time the coffeepot was empty, Madison was stuffed and late for work. Claire was thinking how empty the house was going to be without him.

''McCrea, I'd just about decided you'd went back to Beaumont. Where in hell have you been?''

The question came from Madison's foreman, a big burly man named Ray. He had a head full of salt-and-pepper hair and a mouth full of gold fillings. He'd been a friend of Madison's father, but he liked construction work and when Madison had gone into the business, he'd left his job as an oil driller and went to work as Madison's foreman.

Madison had just pulled up at the site and parked his pickup beside the little camp trailer. Ray had been there when he'd opened the door on the pickup and climbed to the ground.

''Having breakfast with a beautiful brunette. Is that a crime?''

''It is when it makes you late for work,'' Ray retorted.

The grounds were already busy with rumbling cement trucks, shouting workmen, the buzz of power-saws and raps of hammers.

Madison drank in the sights and sounds. To him it represented birth and creation. His blue eyes gleamed as he looked over at his old friend. ''I thought you'd be more sympathetic, since you're the one who's irresistible to women.''

Ray laughed as he clamped his big, thick hand over one of Madison's shoulders. "Well, who was she? Some young chick you picked up last night?"

Grimacing, Madison tugged his hard hat down lower on his forehead. One night stands with women had never been his style. "No. And she wasn't a chick. She's a beautiful, mature lady."

Ray probably wouldn't believe it if he told him he'd spent the bigger part of the night doing his laundry, Madison thought wryly.

"Well, beg my pardon," Ray said. "Where did you meet her? High tea?"

Madison cut him a look that swiftly wiped the humor off the older man's face.

"No, I'm staying at her place. She rents rooms. And no, she doesn't have any more available," he added, already anticipating Ray's next question.

Ray guffawed and slapped Madison on the back. "I can see it's going to be a job getting any work out of you today."

Madison turned and opened the door of the trailer. Ray followed him inside. Madison hung his hard hat on a rack on the wall, then quickly reached for the telephone. "Just tell me what's been going on so far this morning," he said to Ray while punching out a set of numbers. "And I'll tell you what better be done by the end of the day."

"Claire darling, where are you?"

"In here, Liv. In Madison's room."

The older woman appeared in the doorway. She was still wearing her robe and slippers. A matching pink ribbon was tied around her head, holding her gray hair tightly back away from her face.

"Is our handsome houseguest already gone for the day?" she asked.

Claire nodded. "He left hours ago."

Liv entered the room and sat down on the edge of the bed. Claire continued to hang up Madison's shirts and jeans on the rod in the closet.

"I suppose he came down for breakfast," Liv commented. "Did you two have a nice talk?"

"Well, we didn't eat in silence," Claire said. "How did things go with Arthur last night?"

Liv sighed. "Lovely. Just lovely. You know, Claire, the more I try to understand that man the more confused I get. We have two or three wonderful days together and then I can feel him begin to back away again. I think if I even mentioned the word marriage, he'd have a heart attack."

Claire shook out a denim shirt before slipping it onto a hanger. It was one of those expensive western types, making Claire wonder what kind of life-style Madison lived back in Beaumont. She wondered if he had one of those ritzy houses in the affluent part of town. Maybe he threw lots of parties with willing girls. No doubt they'd be much younger than Claire, with pretty faces and long limbs tanned by the Texas sun.

Finding the idea distasteful, she did her best to shake it away and turn her attention to Liv. "Is that what you'd like? To marry Arthur?" Claire asked.

Sighing, Liv rose from the bed and walked over to the windows. "Claire, I was married for thirty-five years. When I lost Frank I thought my life was over. But now—"

Claire noticed a gravity to Liv's features that she'd never seen before. "You do want to marry him."

Liv turned away from the windows and smiled ruefully at Claire. "It's horrible to be alone, Claire," she said, more as an explanation than an answer.

Claire made a dismissive gesture with her hand. "You're not alone, Liv. You have a daughter back in Illinois. You have all your friends here, including me."

Liv slowly shook her head. "It's not the same. You should know that. You were married once."

Claire didn't like being reminded of the biggest mistake in her life. She turned and picked up another one of Madison's shirts from the bed and placed it on a hanger.

"A man isn't everything, Liv. There are other things in life that make a person full, enriched."

"A man isn't, but love is," Liv said pointedly. "Maybe I'm an old foolish woman, but I like to have my hand held just as much as I did when I was a teenager."

"I understand that. I even understand the part about needing to be loved no matter what our age. But sometimes I think a man is incapable of truly loving. I think they all love themselves first and foremost. It's just something that's in their nature."

Liv clucked her tongue as she moved away from the windows. "That's a sad philosophy, Claire. I hate to see someone as young and beautiful as you warped with that kind of thinking."

"You don't know all the circumstances, Liv," Claire pointed out.

"I know one thing," the older woman said while fluffing her gray curls at the back of her neck. "Madison McCrea is gorgeous and you're crazy if you don't take advantage of the fact that he's a guest in your home.''

"I think I'm crazy for not taking a six-week vacation and letting you take care of Madison.''

Liv suddenly laughed, bringing her usually bubbly self back. "Now that isn't a bad idea. Arthur would probably be so jealous, he'd go down on his knees to propose.''

Claire rolled her eyes in disbelief and picked up a pair of jeans. Liv jammed her hands on her small hips and looked calculating.

"You know, Claire, I think that's it. It's about time I let old Arthur know there's other men out there willing and able.''

The older woman quickly sauntered out the door before Claire could ask her just exactly what she intended to do.

Madison didn't arrive home for supper even though Claire waited until nearly sundown to start cooking. Since Liv was gone also, Claire finally decided to take her meal out to the screened-in porch and eat alone. It had turned into a warm day and the air was still pleasant. She sat listening to the lulling night sounds of frogs and insects, wondering what Madison was doing and realizing how much she missed sharing the meal with him.

That was a disturbing idea for Claire because she was used to being alone. She'd even told herself she liked being alone. So why was she so restless now?

It's horrible to be alone. She mulled Liv's words over in her mind, wondering why she should be dwelling on them.

Because you are truly alone, she told herself. She had no family except very distant relatives. She had friends, but they were not the kind who would come running if she were ever in dire need. And Claire supposed Liv was partially right—friends and relatives were not the same as a soul mate.

A long time ago Claire had thought that Larry was a soul mate. She couldn't have been more wrong, and because of it she hadn't been able to trust her judgment of men since. If she could have been so wrong about Larry, what made her think she could be right about another man?

The lasagna she'd made for supper was good, but she ended up eating only one small helping and completely ignored the lemon pie left over from last night.

Two hours later Claire was in her tiny office, a small alcove off the living room, going over a stack of bills when Madison let himself in through the front door.

From behind her desk she watched him cross the living room. He looked very tired and dirty as if his day had been unusually trying. Claire felt the need to go to him.

She hurriedly switched off the lamp and left the office, catching him just as he'd started up the stairs. "Good evening, Madison. I see you made it back."

Madison turned around to see her standing just a few steps away. She looked fresh and beautiful in spite of the late hour. Her long dark hair was brushed loosely around her face and shoulders, and her face had been washed free of makeup.

"Hello," he said warmly. "Sorry I missed supper. I hope you didn't go to extra trouble."

Claire shook her head. "It was no problem. I'll heat a plate for you in the microwave whenever you're ready."

"I wouldn't want to put you out."

She smiled softly and pushed her wayward hair back off her forehead. "If I didn't want to do it, I'd tell you so."

With a broad smile he turned and took the stairs two at a time.

Some minutes later as he sat at the round table on the back porch, he asked, "Where's Liv?"

Claire had just placed his food in front of him. Now she pulled out a chair and took the seat opposite his.

"She's with a friend. Working on needlepoint. Liv keeps herself busy," she explained. Glancing up at him, she realized why she'd missed his presence so much at supper. There was a vitality about the man that made everything around him seem more alive, more important. Seeing his smile reminded her that life was precious, something to be enjoyed and savored.

"Did your crew get a lot done today?" she asked as she sipped her coffee.

He nodded. "More than I'd hoped. Once we get the roofs on, the weather won't present so much of a problem." Chewing a forkful of lasagna, he rested his eyes on her face. "How about you? How did your day go?"

Claire shrugged. "About like usual." She wasn't about to tell him that she'd thought about him all day. "My life is very slow. I purposely make it that way."

"So you're avoiding all those stress-related nasties like ulcers and high blood pressure."

"No. I just like living in a laid-back fashion. I never was one of those women who pined for a high-powered career. I guess that makes me look like I need a shot of ambition. Especially to someone like you."

His brows lifted with wry speculation. "Why do you say that?"

She turned her palm up on the tabletop. "Well, you're obviously an ambitious man. I'm sure you notice it when someone isn't."

He shook his head. "I think you're confusing laziness with something else. Just because you don't want a career outside your home doesn't mean you're lazy. From what I've seen around here, you're far from lazy."

Smiling more to herself than at him, she picked up her coffee cup. "I suppose I'm more like my mother than I thought. She wanted nothing more than to be a wife and mother."

But her mother had had a drunk for a husband, Madison thought ruefully. Marriage hadn't worked for her mother, and it hadn't worked for Claire.

"You said you weren't the marrying kind," he reminded her of their conversation in the Laundromat. Already that seemed like a long time ago. Already he felt as if he knew her well.

She laughed softly while her eyes roamed his face. The fact that his skin was so tanned made his blue eyes even that much bluer. There was a faint shadow of a beard on his face, dark brown whiskers mixed with a few russet ones. She wondered how he would react in the morning if she perched herself on the side of the bathtub and watched while he shaved.

"That's right, I did say that. Because that's the way I feel now. I used to believe in all those dreams about a two-story house, picket fence and a swing set in the backyard. But that dream left me a long time ago. Just about the same time Larry did. That's not to say I wouldn't like a baby." She grimaced, then sipped her coffee. "I just haven't figured out how to go about getting one without having a man involved."

Madison swallowed a piece of garlic bread. "I'm afraid that's biologically impossible."

Claire frowned mockingly. "Yes, I know. That's why you don't see any babies around here."

Wondering how on earth their conversation had come around to this topic, Claire got up from the table in hopes of changing it. "I'll get the pie from the refrigerator."

Madison watched her go, surprised to find that she'd saved him something for supper. He'd half expected her to be put out with him for being so late. But don't go thinking she's an understanding woman, he told himself. She's just like you. She doesn't want to be tied to anyone. She might want a baby, but she doesn't want a man. And you fit into the last category, Madison.

He contemplated the idea of Claire Deupree pregnant and felt a smile spreading across his face. He wouldn't mind the task of getting her pregnant. Wouldn't mind it at all.

Chapter Five

Claire returned with the pie and refilled Madison's coffee cup.

"Where will you go when you get through with this job?" she asked. "Do you already have another one lined up?"

Madison nodded. "Shreveport. A convenience store. But that's closer to home and the job won't take long."

So he would be back home in Beaumont, she thought. She wondered for the second time what kind of life he led there. "Is there ever a time when you don't have a job waiting?"

He pushed aside his empty plate. "Not really. But I do take time off now and then. Money isn't everything."

"Do you spend much time with your family?"

Madison shrugged, his expression evasive as he took the pie she offered him. "I see my mother more than any of them. She thinks she needs to keep an eye on her baby son.''

Claire smiled at the idea his words presented. ''It must be nice to have family.''

''Why do you say that? Don't you have any living relatives?''

She shook her head slowly. ''Only very distant relatives living down south. I was close to the aunt who owned this house, but she died of a stroke several years ago.''

''Did she have a husband or children?''

Claire grimaced. ''She used to have a husband. But that was many years ago. One day he just up and left her, said he was tired of being married. Aunt Rose never got over it.''

Madison looked at her as he sliced the pie. ''Do you know what ever happened to him?''

Claire shook her head. ''Not really. We heard rumors that he'd been killed out in California, but I don't hold much stock in them. I really can't say what happened to him, but I hated him for what he did to Aunt Rose. She was a fine, lovely woman. She didn't deserve what she got from him.''

Madison pondered her words as he chewed. ''The women in your family haven't been very lucky with men, have they?''

She made a sound of bitter disbelief as she splashed a bit more coffee into her cup. ''Is that what you have to have—luck?''

A sheepish expression came over Madison's face. ''I don't know. But all men aren't bad. At least I'm not a stinker.''

"Oh really? Gosh, let me look at you. You're very rare indeed."

"Claire," he said, clucking his tongue at her. "You're not really all that cynical are you?"

The corners of her mouth lifted into a wan smile. "Not cynical, just smart."

"You must not be a man hater, because you were dating the boor."

"On the contrary, I like men, as long as they're at least this far away." She indicated the distance between them, which was the width of the table.

He eyed that, then settled his blue eyes on her face. "That's playing too safe for me. Nothing can happen at that distance."

She knew he was teasing her, even though the look on his face wasn't a humorous one. She laughed softly. "That's the whole point, Mr. McCrea."

Without warning, he got up and came around the table to where she was. Surprised, Claire stared up at him.

He reached for her hand that was on the tabletop. "How about this distance? Don't you think this is much nicer?"

Before she could answer, he pressed her hand between both his and pure sensation rocketed through Claire's body. "I think you would be much nicer if you backed away," she replied.

A slow, lopsided grin spread across his face. "I said I wasn't a stinker. I didn't say anything about being nice."

Claire took a deep breath, willing her runaway heart to slow itself. "I'm your landlady, remember?"

Madison tugged on her hand until she was standing only inches away from him. "You're a woman first," he said in a low voice.

"But you shouldn't think of me that way."

"I'd have to be blind not to."

A mocking laugh boiled up inside Claire, but by the time it passed her tight throat it was more like a gurgle of disbelief. "I'm older than you are. I have gray hairs and wrinkles."

He chuckled, causing his warm breath to fan her cheeks. "Your hair is as dark as midnight," he said, lifting one of his hands away from hers and touching the curls on her shoulder. "And the only wrinkles I see are the ones on your forehead from frowning at me." His fingers lifted and traced a path from eyebrow to eyebrow.

Claire felt herself shivering; her knees were ridiculously weak. She wanted to tell him to stop touching her, but nothing would come out of her mouth.

"Why don't you let me kiss you behind the ear, Claire? I promise it'll be better with me."

She gasped. "You're an arrogant man!"

He gave her another daunting grin as he drawled, "And you're a beautiful woman."

She swallowed as she looked up and met his eyes. The taunting gleam in them told her how much he was enjoying the moment.

"I don't get involved with men," she reminded him in a husky voice. "And you're not the marrying kind."

One of his shoulders moved with a neglible shrug. "Marriage has nothing to do with this."

"And just what is *this?*" Claire asked.

"Just a little closeness between friends."

Her delicate brows arched upward. "Are we friends?"

His head bent down and the quivering inside Claire increased two-fold.

"I want to think we're going to become good friends," he murmured, his face only inches away from hers.

Claire's hand tightened on his. It had to. Otherwise, she was sure her legs were going to give way and she'd slide to the floor like a pat of melted butter.

"And just what do you call good friends?" she asked. Her shallow breathing could be heard in her voice and she wondered why she couldn't be as cool and unaffected with Madison as she had been with Saul.

He rolled his eyes thoughtfully, then pushed his hand through her hair. Once the silky strands had slid through his fingers he settled his hand on her bare shoulder.

"Good friends are two people who are attached to each other by mutual affection."

Attached. Affection. The words sounded far too serious for Claire. "I could never see us being attached."

Madison certainly could. In all sorts of different ways. "Right now I'm just asking for one little kiss."

"Madison—"

His name whispered out on her breath as his hand pushed back the cloud of hair against her neck. Claire stood immobilized, not knowing whether she wanted to jerk away or throw her arms around him.

Before she could make up her mind, his nose was nuzzling the side of her neck, sending delicious little goosebumps down her back.

"You smell good, Claire. Like a sultry gardenia," he whispered.

"Madison, don't do—"

"Do what? This?"

He kissed her then, just behind the earlobe. Claire wasn't sure whether she was still standing or if she were somehow floating.

Her hands reached up and grabbed the front of his shirt. Madison slipped his arm around her waist and drew her closer. She shivered outwardly and her eyes closed as his lips brushed down her jaw, then up and across her cheek and nose.

Claire was so mesmerized by then that her face was tilting up to his, her mouth searching for his tantalizing lips. She wanted him to kiss her even though she knew it would be like throwing herself into a raging fire.

She was wondering what the consequences would be when suddenly she felt his arms move from around her and his head lift back up to its normal position.

"You're right, Claire. We're not even friends yet. A kiss would be asking too much of you."

Dazed, she felt her eyelids fluttering open. Her heart was pounding and her cheeks were flushed. He knew she'd wanted him to kiss her. They both knew it. But for some reason he'd changed his mind and backed away. Maybe when it came right down to it, he was as wary of women as she was of men, she thought. Her eyes darted up to his face.

"I . . . think you're right, Madison."

There was a wry expression on his face as he walked over to the screen door leading to the back steps. Claire took a deep breath and reached for his dirty dishes. She had to do something as she attempted to pull her scattered senses back together.

Just as she was carrying the dishes into the kitchen, the telephone rang. It was a man requesting to speak to Madison.

She called out to him and he came quickly, thanking her as she handed the telephone to him.

"Yeah, Ray, what is it?" Madison spoke to the caller.

Claire began to rinse Madison's plate and silverware. As soon as she had them in the drainer she was going to leave the kitchen so he could finish his conversation in privacy. She didn't want him thinking she was trying to eavesdrop, and she certainly didn't want him thinking she wanted to hang around and finish where they'd left off.

"No, I want to check on the price of that drywalling before we order," he spoke into the telephone. "Did the power company ever show up?"

Claire slipped past him and out of the room. Since it was becoming very late, she intended to go straight up to her room and to bed, but Liv walked in the front door just as Claire was climbing the stairs.

"Hi, sweetie," the older woman greeted. "Going to bed?"

Claire nodded. "How was your evening? Did you get much accomplished on your needlepoint?"

"Oh, some. We wound up gossiping most of the evening away. Janie is on top of the world. Her daughter just found out she's pregnant with her first child."

"That's nice," Claire said and meant it. She'd meant it earlier this evening, too, when she'd told Madison she would like a child of her own. This past year she'd been more aware of that biological clock ticking away inside her. She'd also been sadly aware that it was futile to think of herself as a mother. To be a mother, she also needed to be a wife, and she could never open herself up to that kind of pain again.

Liv joined Claire on the staircase. "Where's our guest? In bed?"

Claire shook her head. "In the kitchen on the telephone."

Liv gave her a sly look. "Were you two having a little late night snack together?"

Claire began to climb the steps, knowing Liv would follow. "I heated Madison's supper for him. He had to work late."

"Hmm, you never heated my supper."

"You never had to work late."

Liv laughed. "Has he asked you out yet?"

Claire tossed a frown over her shoulder at the older woman. "Liv, the man is here to work, nothing more." Thank God Liv hadn't come in earlier and found her in Madison's arms, Claire thought. She'd already have the two of them having a torrid affair.

"He thinks you're pretty. I can tell by the way he looks at you."

"That doesn't mean he'll ask me out," Claire reasoned, her voice growing weary.

"Well, that doesn't mean you'll turn him down, does it? I mean if he asks you—Claire, you'd be crazy to turn him down!"

They were on the landing now. Claire went straight to her bedroom door and opened it. She didn't intend to keep up this conversation tonight.

"Liv, you know how I stand on this subject. Even if such a thing came up, it wouldn't mean anything. I wouldn't let it. Besides, Madison is not from here. After a few weeks he'll be leaving and we'll never see him again."

Liv walked past Claire and started into her own bedroom, but just before she shut the door behind her, she said, "One of these days love is going to hit you, and when it does, things won't seem so black-and-white anymore."

"Goodnight, Liv," Claire said with a sigh.

Liv was a bubbly romantic, Claire thought a few minutes later as she undressed. The woman looked at everything with rose-colored glasses and expected Claire to do the same.

After pulling a pale yellow gown over her head, Claire smoothed it down over her hips. Her image was reflected in the cheval mirror standing a few feet away.

Did she really look beautiful to Madison? He'd said so, but she knew from experience that men could say anything and make it sound sincere if it gained them what they wanted.

But what exactly did Madison want from her? she asked herself. An affair? Just the word made her turn crimson. Madison was a sexy man. A lot of women would feel flattered to have his attention. But Claire knew that no matter how sexy or good-looking, she couldn't have an affair with any man. She wasn't cut out for it. She knew that if she ever let herself get that close to a man again, her heart would invariably become involved right along with her body. And when the affair was over, she'd be alone with an empty feeling just as she was now.

The next morning Claire hurried around the kitchen, looking bright and beautiful in a yellow jumpsuit, even though she'd lain awake most of the night examining her growing attraction for Madison.

Friends. Madison said he'd like to be her good friend. Maybe she could handle that, she thought. Millions of people had friends of the opposite sex. But the way he'd said it made it sound much more meaningful than a person you chatted with over the backyard fence, or borrowed a cup of sugar from.

How had he put it? Two people attached to each other by mutual affection. That sounded more like a pair of lovers to her.

Claire was so obviously deep in thought that she didn't hear Madison when he came into the kitchen. He watched her pouring batter onto a hot waffle iron. Across the counter a man on the radio was predicting a warm, muggy day. It was a homey sight and he suddenly thought of his brother, Mitch, and how happy he was being a husband and a father. But then Mitch was successful at any endeavor he tried. Whereas Madison had always been viewed as the rebel with the uncertain future.

"Good morning, Claire."

Startled at the sound of his voice, she whirled around, nearly dropping the bowl of batter she was holding.

"Madison! You startled me."

He gave her a lazy smile and Claire's eyes went directly to his mouth. Last night he'd been so close to kissing her that she'd wondered over and over what it would have been like if he had.

"Sorry. Am I early?"

Claire suddenly remembered the waffles and turned to shut the lid over the batter. "No, you timed it perfectly. These waffles will be done in just a minute."

"Mmm, waffles," he repeated as he went over to the coffeepot. "Liv didn't say anything about you cooking waffles for breakfast."

"That's because Liv doesn't know everything about me."

He laughed softly and Claire discovered he'd come to stand beside her instead of seating himself at the table.

"I'll bet that's true."

Claire busied herself with stirring the batter, even though it didn't need it.

Madison said, "I like this room, Claire. In fact, I like this whole house. It makes me think of slower, gentler times."

Surprised by his nostalgic comment, Claire looked up at him. "I would have thought you'd be looking at it through an engineer's eyes. There's probably a lot to be said for its structuring."

"These old houses built around the turn of the century are fascinating. So much manual labor went into them. It probably took much more time to build this house than it will for my crew to finish the motel."

The waffles were ready to eat. Claire carried them over to his plate, and he followed. As he moved beside her to take his seat, Claire caught the scent of his cologne.

Her eyes felt drawn to his face. She saw that it was cleanly shaven, the whiskers she'd noticed last night gone. Right now if he should rub his jaw against her face and neck it would be soft and warm. So would his lips.

Their eyes met and clung. Claire's heart reacted like a racehorse just out of the gates.

"Thank you, Claire."

"For what?"

One corner of his mouth crooked upward. "For being so nice to me."

"I'm nice to everyone."

That wasn't exactly what he wanted from her. He wanted her to treat him as though he were someone special. "Have you thought about what I said last night?"

Claire's mind raced back and forth over the things they'd said to each other. "About what?"

"About us being friends."

"Uh, well . . . yes."

"Yes, we'll be friends? Or yes, you thought about it?"

She drew in a deep breath and let it out slowly. "Yes, I thought about it."

Before he could question her further, she stepped past him and hurried back to the waffle iron. She gave the batter a few whips, then poured it onto the hot griddle. Behind her, Madison sat down and began to butter his waffles. Every few moments his eyes were drawn to Claire.

Madison knew that he disturbed Claire. He could see that every time he came near her. Yet he wasn't quite sure why he disturbed her. She was either attracted to him, or she was so gun-shy after being hurt by a man that she just didn't want one getting close.

"I suppose we could be friends, Madison," he heard her saying. "They say there's nothing like having a true friend."

Since Claire had her back to him, she was unaware of the surprised look on Madison's face. He'd almost convinced himself that she was going to point out she was the landlady and he was the boarder and that was as far as it would go. She couldn't know how much she'd just pleased him with her unexpected words.

"That's exactly the way I see it," he said.

Claire turned around to see that he was pouring syrup over the plate of waffles. "After all," Claire went on, "we're both mature adults and we both know how we stand on things. Friendship between us would be nice." And safe, she silently added.

Madison noticed her smile was nervous and the tone of her voice was almost too eager. Madison got the impression she was afraid he was suddenly going to invite her up to his bed. He'd certainly thought about it, he silently admitted. Every time he looked at her he thought about it. But it seemed as though the more the thought entered his head, the more he pushed it away. There was something different about Claire. He'd sensed it that first day he'd met her, and last night when he'd had his arms around her waist, her soft cheek against his, he'd known she was more than something different. He'd felt the vulnerable quiver in her body and he'd suddenly known that he didn't want to take advantage of it. A rush of protectiveness had filled him and the feeling had been so different, so out of character for him, that it had left him stunned.

Claire must have thought he was out of his mind. He'd come on to her, asking her for a kiss and just about the time she was ready to give him one, he'd backed away like a teenager with cold feet.

"Very nice," he agreed. He picked up his coffee cup and thrust it toward her. "Come here and make a toast with me. I think we deserve that."

Claire wasn't really sure about any of this, or even if deep down he was sincere about being her friend, but for now she was going to go along with him. After all, last night he could have kissed her. He could have taken advantage of that weak moment she'd stood within the circle of his arms. But he hadn't.

"Just a moment. Let me get my waffles first," she told him. After she'd deposited her food on her plate, she lifted her coffee cup to his. Her smile was easy this time as he clanked his cup against hers and smiled back at her.

"To our newfound friendship," he said softly. "May it grow and flourish."

"Friends," she murmured in agreement.

Later that afternoon Claire had just come back from a long jog when Madison's pickup pulled to a stop in front of the house. To Claire's dismay he caught her hosing down her bare arms and legs.

"Have you decided to give up traditional baths for the garden hose?"

Striding up the sidewalk, he gave her a grin. Not because she was hosing herself with cold water, but because he was enjoying the sight of her in a pair of jogging shorts. She had long, shapely legs right down to her trim ankles and bare feet.

"Not exactly. I've been out jogging and I'm hot."

Madison could see that she was overheated. Her cheeks were flushed red and the bangs falling over her forehead were damp with perspiration. Funny how none of that took away from her beauty, he thought.

Claire glanced curiously at him as he took a seat on the porch floor. "What are you doing home in the middle of the afternoon?"

She called it home. It was a word he'd shied away from connecting with other women. But somehow hearing Claire say it didn't make it seem all that threatening.

"I found a good stopping place for me. And Ray is keeping the rest of the crew in line."

She tossed the hose aside and went to turn off the spigot. Since her feet were wet she sat down on the porch a few feet away from Madison to wait for them to dry before putting her shoes back on.

"That must be nice," she mused aloud. "Being a boss and being able to take off whenever you want."

"Whoa now," he said with a chuckle. "I don't get to take off anytime I like. Just sometimes. Besides, you're your own boss. You're not really tied down."

Claire drew her knees up to her chest and stared out across the front yard. She'd mowed it about four days ago, but already the rain showers had it sprouting back up. Claire didn't strive for a perfect yard. Her house wasn't perfect and she wasn't perfect, so she didn't see any sense in killing herself for a pad of perfect Bermuda. She'd learned the hard way that no matter how much a person tried to be perfect, it was never enough to please everyone.

"I don't make the money you do, either," she reasoned, then reached behind her for her shoes. One by one she pulled them on her feet and tied the laces. "I think I'll drag out the lawn mower. It's at least two hours till supper time."

The lawn mower! All day Madison had shuffled and jiggled his work load just so he could get home early and spend some time with her. Now she was saying she was going to mow the lawn! He had to do something fast.

"The lawn looks fine to me," Madison said, watching Claire get to her feet. Her legs were slick, shapely and doing sinful things to his mind. It was strange how this woman could bring out such contradictory feelings in him such as lust and protectiveness. It didn't make sense. "I was thinking it would be nice if you and I went out somewhere this evening. It will save you from cooking."

"Go out?" His suggestion took her by complete surprise. It showed on her face. "Go out where?"

Shrugging, he got to his feet. "Doesn't matter to me. It might be fun to drive out to Beaver Lake. I'm sure you've seen it hundreds of times, but I haven't. Not close up. Would you like to go? We could get a hamburger afterward."

"A hamburger?" She knew she was echoing his words, but she hadn't expected an invitation from him.

Even if she had, she wouldn't have expected one this soon.

"Well, you can have steak if you'd rather. I'm not stingy. I just happen to like hamburgers."

Claire felt a blush sting her cheeks. "That wasn't what I meant. I just didn't—why do you want to go out?"

He smiled at her in a way that was hard for Claire to decipher. "Since we've decided to be friends, I thought it would give us a chance to get to know each other better."

Liv was already gone for the evening with Arthur. If she and Madison stayed here, she'd really be more alone with him than if they went out. And to be honest, it had been a long time since she'd had a leisurely outing.

"Do you like to swim?" she asked suddenly.

Madison was more than surprised by her question. He'd really expected a cool no and a reminder that she was his landlady. "I love to swim," he answered.

"Good. Then I'll pack some sandwiches and we can swim and picnic. What do you think?"

Madison could think of nothing he'd like better than to see Claire in a swimsuit. "I think I'll be ready in five minutes. How about you?"

She laughed as she started into the house, with Madison right on her heels. "You better give me ten, unless you want to help me make the sandwiches."

"I will. I'm a great sandwich maker. I'll meet you in the kitchen as soon as I change."

Claire watched him bound up the staircase, and felt her spirits suddenly lift. It had been so long since she'd allowed herself to enjoy a man's company. And Madison was sweet and sexy. Being with him was like flirting with danger. It made her heart beat faster, her cheeks flush, her mind whirl. She was a woman, she reasoned with herself as she hurriedly stripped and stepped into a swimsuit. It wouldn't hurt to enjoy a picnic with a man. A woman had that right once in a while, didn't she?

Madison rummaged through his things and found a pair of cutoff blue jeans. While pulling them on, he examined his motives for asking Claire to go out with him.

He'd asked her to be his friend, and he'd been sincere about that. Now wasn't the right time or the right place to let himself become more involved than that. Starting today, and for the next six weeks, he'd simply enjoy having her company. That was all there was to it.

Chapter Six

Claire was already in the kitchen when Madison came downstairs. She was wearing a pair of skimpy white shorts over a red swimsuit. Her back was to him and he watched her long, dark hair brush against her bare skin as she moved at the kitchen counter. Madison realized he'd never met a woman who'd affected him in such a physical way before. It was enough to scare a man.

Down through the years Madison had known a few beautiful women but none of them had stirred him like Claire. He wondered if it was because she was older, more mature, more womanly than those others. Whatever the case, he longed to go to her now, draw her against him and slide his hands across the creamy smooth skin of her back.

"What would you like for me to do?" he asked.

Claire glanced over her shoulder at him and suddenly had to bite her tongue to keep from bursting out with laughter. He was wearing a pair of cutoff jeans and a plain white T-shirt, both of which looked great on him. It was his feet that had quickly caught her attention. He was wearing a pair of black cowboy boots that came nearly to his knees.

Madison saw the direction her eyes had taken and smiled cockily. "What's the matter? Don't you like my footwear?"

Claire carefully cleared her throat. "Well, it's not really beachwear. Is that all you have with you?"

"I have two other choices. A pair of brown cowboy boots or a pair of lace-up work boots. What do you think?"

"I think we'd better make a stop in town," she said as tactfully as she could manage.

"My feelings are hurt now, but I never was a sulky boy. I'll get over it. Do you want me to make the sandwiches?"

"First tell me if you like mayonnaise or mustard."

He walked up behind her and peered over her shoulder. "What kind of lunch meat?"

"Pickle loaf and bologna."

"Mayonnaise," he said, taking the knife from her hand. "You go on and do something else."

Madison began to smear mayonnaise over the bread slices on the counter. Claire watched him for a moment, then hurried over to the refrigerator and pulled out two ice trays.

"Would you like to take cola or lemonade?" she asked, glancing over her shoulder at him.

"You choose. I'm not particular."

Claire made lemonade. By the time she was finished, Madison had four sandwiches put together.

They packed them, along with several pieces of fruit and a bag of chips, into a wicker hamper. Madison carried it to his pickup, while Claire carried two large beach towels and a small transistor radio.

"Do you really think I need shoes?" Madison asked as he drove them through town. "I doubt anyone will notice my boots."

Claire could not hold her laughter this time. "No one will notice? You've got to be kidding? The bottom part of you looks like you stepped out of a B western. Pull over at this next discount store and I'll buy you a pair of shoes."

"If you think it's that necessary."

Claire rolled her eyes. "It's more than necessary. It's my duty."

At the next block Madison flipped on the turn signal and pulled into a wide parking area.

Claire slipped a white blouse over the top of her swimsuit and grabbed up her purse. "I'll be right back," she promised, quickly scooting out the door.

"But Claire, you'll need money and you don't know what—" he started to protest.

She waved away his words and started toward the store. "I know everything I need to know," she called back to him.

Five minutes later she came out of the store carrying a paper sack. Madison eyed it warily as she got back into the truck. "Are you sure there's a pair of shoes in there? It looks awfully flat to me."

Claire gave him a smug smile and pulled out a pair of red rubber thongs. Madison looked at them as if they were two foreign objects.

"Thongs? I was expecting tennis shoes, at least!"

Claire gave him a dry look. "We're going to be swimming, not playing basketball."

"Yes, but those are wimpy. Do I look like a thong man? Besides, if I wear those you can see my feet and that'll be embarrassing because my feet are ugly."

Claire didn't believe him for a minute. There couldn't be an ugly spot on his body and she seriously doubted he'd ever been embarrassed in front of a woman.

"I'm wearing thongs and it's not bothering me," she pointed out.

Madison started the engine and pulled back out onto the main street, but not before he'd given Claire's feet and legs a thorough looking over. Her feet were small, the toenails short and painted bright red. Her legs were lightly tanned like the rest of her body. He wondered what they would feel like against his, then quickly told himself to forget it. Once he got to thinking about her legs, he'd get to thinking about the rest of her body and then his common sense would crumble like a soft cookie.

"Yeah, but you've got pretty feet," he reasoned.

She looked at the black cowboy boots covering his feet and legs. They were obviously expensive with intricate stitchings and red insets on the upper parts. "I didn't realize that beneath your jeans you were so flamboyant."

It didn't dawn on Claire just how her words sounded until Madison took his attention off the traffic and gave her a wicked smile. "All you had to do was ask, and I would have been glad to show you."

"That's not what I meant, Madison!"

He laughed and settled back, resting his arm casually on top of the seat. "Of course you didn't. I'm just being a rascal."

Claire crossed her legs and looked over at him. If he was a rascal, he was a gorgeous one. His brown hair was blowing from the breeze coming through the open window. It was a warm glossy color, thick and unruly. Two or three locks kept falling forward and brushing his brows. He didn't seem to notice or be pestered by it. But then she wasn't surprised. He was not a man enamored with himself. She doubted his looks rarely crossed his mind, or if they did he didn't think of himself as handsome.

"Are you known for being a rascal?" she asked, a little smile etched around her lips.

"No!" he said with mock indignation. "Ray, my foreman, is a rascal. I'm known as a good and trusty scout." He held up his hand in a Boy Scout salute, which made Claire groan.

"Oh please. I'm not that gullible."

"I beg your pardon! I was a great scout. Mama was a den mother for six straight years. She felt it her duty since Mitch and I were both scouts. You would think six years was enough to kill her. But she's working as a den mother now. She loves little boys and I suppose it gives her something to do while Dad is away making oil deals." Madison glanced over at Claire. "What about you? I'll bet you were a cute little Brownie, weren't you?"

The smile fell from Claire's face. She looked away from him and out the window. "No. I didn't belong to any children's organizations."

In reality, Claire's father's drinking had seeped into every aspect of her life. She or her mother could never plan outings or parties. Claire could never invite friends over. The few times she had, her father had arrived home drunk, humiliating them all. By the time Claire was nine years old, she'd realized with uncommon maturity that her life was not like those of her schoolmates.

Madison instinctively knew that he'd said something wrong, but he didn't know what. One minute they'd been laughing and the next minute she had this strained, faraway look on her face.

"Claire? Is something wrong?"

His question interrupted her memories. She turned her head to look at him. Would he understand if she tried to tell him? She'd never discussed her childhood with anyone. It had always been too painful.

"I was just imagining what it would have been like if my mother had been a troop leader. Can't you see a group of little girls listening to an adult talk about good manners and morals while a drunk man staggers into the room spewing out vulgar language?" Claire shook her head. "I didn't live like you, Madison."

No, she hadn't, he thought grimly.

A smile suddenly brightened her face. "But let's not talk about such things. The day is too beautiful. So tell me how you like your thongs. Truthfully this time."

Madison understood that she wanted to change the subject and he would oblige her. He wanted this time with her to be fun and lighthearted. He sensed that she'd never really had that many carefree times in her life, and he wanted to think that he could give them to her.

"Truthfully," he said, "they're perfect. Lightweight, air-conditioned, washable and when we get back home I can use them for house shoes."

Claire laughed softly. "A practical man."

Chapter Seven

The highway leading out to Beaver Lake was narrow, steep and winding. Since it was the major highway leading into Eureka Springs from the west, it was nearly always busy with traffic. Madison drove slowly while Claire pointed out different things she thought might interest him.

There were only a handful of swimmers when Claire and Madison parked and picked their way down to the beach.

"This place is beautiful," Madison remarked as they deposited their things on the ground.

For as far as the eye could see, the lake spread like silver fingers between green mountains. The picnic and camping areas were carpeted with grass and shaded with tall hardwood trees. In the distance skiboats and brightly colored sailboards bobbed on the sparkling water.

"The water will feel beautiful, too!" Claire exclaimed. Quickly she shed her blouse and shorts and ran to the water's edge. It sprayed around her legs as she entered it, making her squeal with carefree delight.

Smiling at her enthusiasm, Madison tossed his T-shirt aside and quickly followed her. To him the water was like ice. Halfway up to his knees, he gulped and stopped in his tracks.

Claire, who by now was already up to her neck in it, called out to him. "I thought you said you weren't wimpy?"

"This stuff has come off a glacier!"

Claire laughed. "Dive in all at once and you won't feel a thing."

He gave her a mocking look. "Of course I won't feel anything. I'll be numb."

Claire came striding back toward him, rising up out of the water, Madison thought, like a dark, beautiful nymph. The top of her breasts were exposed above the red fabric. Droplets of water ran down the valley between them, making Madison wish his eyes could follow their course as they disappeared from his view.

"You might as well come in," she said tauntingly. "Or I'm going to splash water all over you."

As Madison looked at her body, half submerged in water, he decided he wasn't as cold as he'd first thought. "All right. You asked for this."

With a huge lunge he landed somewhere near Claire. Water spewed up from the impact of his body and drenched Claire. She laughed and slicked back her wet hair while Madison coughed and spluttered.

"See. I told you you wouldn't feel anything," she told him.

"Woman, if I get pneumonia you're going to have to nurse me night and day."

Claire merely laughed. "You're a tough Texan, aren't you? Come swim with me out to the buoys."

The buoys she was speaking of were bright red floaters strung together with cable. They marked the restricted swimming area from the rest of the lake, warning swimmers that the water was becoming deep, and warning boaters to stay away from the swimmers.

Madison looked from where they were standing out to the buoys. She was talking about a fair distance and he hadn't swum in a long time. He hoped he was as fit as she thought he was.

"You don't ask much from a man, do you?" he asked.

Claire shook her head, thinking this was the first time in a long time that she'd asked anything from a man. But for some reason she felt herself growing close to Madison. She actually wanted to be with him, wanted to talk with him. It was a brand-new feeling for Claire.

"Not at all," she said, pushing out, then gliding stroke by stroke through the cool water.

Madison followed, his long limbs catching up to her quickly. They swam almost in unison, side by side, the sun on their heads and water rippling over their bodies. Both were out of breath by the time they reached the buoys. Laughing, they grabbed onto the cable to float and rest.

"You must be in great shape, lady. My lungs feel like they're going to burst."

Claire was just as winded as he, but she savored the compliment anyway. "That's because I'm pushing the lawn mower while you're reading blueprints."

"Oh yeah? Well, tomorrow you can go to work in my place and I'll mow the lawn."

Claire smiled with pure pleasure as she floated on her back and turned up her face to the sky. "Your men probably wouldn't want to work for me," she told him.

"I don't know about that, but they'd sure enjoy looking at you."

It was hard for Claire to believe that he thought her pretty, a woman whom men found attractive. She'd never thought of herself in that context, especially the last few years as she'd entered her thirties. What did he see when he looked at her? She longed to know but knew she would be better off not asking. They were friends, nothing more.

"Shall we swim back? I get spooked out here in the deep water if I stay very long."

"Whenever you're ready," he agreed.

They swam slower this time. Claire was tired by the time they could touch bottom without being in over their heads.

"I really think that bit of exercise deserves a glass of lemonade, don't you?" Madison suggested.

Claire followed him out of the water and up to their things. "Yes, I do. Do you want to spread our towels here in the sun or take them to the shade?"

"This is okay with me. I'm still numb."

Unthinkingly, Claire reached over and gave his upper arm a pinch, which made him yelp. Claire laughed. "Just as I thought," she said. "You were lying."

With great exaggeration he rubbed the spot she'd pinched. "I knew you were a dangerous woman the first time I saw you."

Claire picked up a towel and spread it across the sand. "You didn't think any such thing."

She glanced up from her task to see that he was silently laughing at her.

"Yes, I did," he insisted. "I thought you were dangerous and Liv was a nymphomaniac."

She made a face at him as he spread his towel and sat down close beside her. "If you thought that, what made you stay?" she asked, trying to keep from laughing at the idea of Liv being a nymphomaniac. The older woman would love hearing herself described as such.

That was easy enough to answer, Madison thought. He'd taken one look at Claire and knew he would stay even if his room had been in a tent. But he couldn't tell her that. She'd take it the wrong way and probably get all cool and prim on him, and he liked her much better this way.

"I only had fifteen more minutes to find a room before I had to be back on the job. I didn't want to look anymore," he lied.

"Oh I see," she said. "So you decided to be brave about it."

"I'm always brave."

"Really?"

No. But he wanted her to think so. "Aren't men supposed to be?"

"Just like women are supposed to be submissive," she responded.

Madison loved the idea of Claire being submissive to his desire. Just the thought of it made this great manly feeling well up inside him. Is that the way it would feel if he were in love and married? he wondered.

Claire reached into the picnic hamper and pulled out two glasses. Madison shook his disturbing thoughts away and picked up the thermos of lemonade lying beside him.

"I'll pour," he told her.

"Mmm, that goes down good in this heat," she said, swallowing the cool, tart drink.

Madison nodded his agreement as he watched a family picnicking some thirty yards down the beach from them. There were two children, a blond boy and a dark-headed girl. Presently they were having a tussle over an air mattress.

"Why doesn't she box him over the head?" Madison spoke his thoughts aloud. "He's pulling her hair. And look at their parents. They don't even know anything is going on."

Claire laughed as she watched the scene. "From what I've gathered, that's what brothers and sisters are supposed to do. I'm sure you and your brother did, especially if he's only a year older than you."

"Yes, but we were boys. You're not supposed to be mean to little girls."

Claire had to laugh again. "Lord help you if you ever have a daughter. She'll never stand a chance in the world."

Madison suddenly turned his attention back to Claire. "Why do you say that?"

"Because you'll have her spoiled rotten. And then you'll learn that little girls can be just as mischievous and mean as little boys."

As if to underscore Claire's point the boy's loud yelps had them both turning their heads to see the girl kicking her brother hard on the shins.

Madison chuckled with amusement as he watched the boy surrender and let his sister have the air mattress.

"I used to pray for a brother," Claire admitted as she crossed her legs in Indian fashion. "I had this foolish idea that a brother would have protected me from Dad's drinking."

Madison studied Claire thoughtfully as he drank his lemonade. "Did your father abuse you?"

Claire shook her head. "Not physically, if that's what you mean. It was the mental anguish that I wanted to be protected from. I don't know why I thought a brother would help." She met his blue eyes and was surprised to find that it eased her heart to talk to him. There was a tenderness in his eyes that she'd never seen in Larry's, but then her ex-husband had not been a compassionate man. Something told her that Madison would be.

Madison said, "When my brother and I were small, we fought like cats and dogs, but by the time we were teenagers it didn't matter anymore."

Curious, Claire asked, "What does that mean?"

He shrugged and looked away from her. For some odd reason Claire had the urge to reach over and touch his arm.

"I found myself fighting more with my father than with my brother," he said.

"Why was that?" she asked. It didn't cross her mind that she was being too personal. He was no longer a stranger.

Madison let out a heavy breath as he stared out over the lake. "Because Dad was never satisfied with just me. He always wanted me to be more like Mitch. Mitch does this so well, why don't you try it? he'd say. Or Mitch doesn't have any problem with history, why do you? I wanted to yell at him that I wasn't Mitch, that I was me."

This time Claire did reach over and touch his arm. Shocked to find her fingers on his arm, Madison turned his face back to her.

"Why didn't you?" she asked softly.

He shrugged as though it no longer mattered. But Claire got the impression that he was only trying to disguise a hurt that ran very deep.

"Because it would have been futile," he tried to explain. "I couldn't be like Mitch. There wasn't any use in trying."

"I'm glad you didn't try," she said huskily. "Because I like you as you are. Madison McCrea, a good and trusty scout, and a little bit of a rascal."

No one had said anything to him that meant as much. He felt a lump in his throat and wondered what in God's name was coming over him. Before he knew what he was doing his hands were on her shoulders and he was pushing her back against the towel and the grass.

She stared up at him with her dark hazel eyes and Madison felt something stir deep inside him. "Friends can share kisses, can't they?"

"I don't know," she murmured. "I've never had a friend like you."

With a little groan he leaned over her, settling his mouth over her red-ripe lips. Kissing Claire was just as he'd thought it would be—mind-consuming. As he tasted her softness, her sweetness, he forgot everything, even the fact that they had an audience. It wasn't until he caught the near sound of children's laughter that he lifted his head and ended the kiss.

Looking down at her he saw that her breasts were rising and falling with rapid, shallow movements. There was a strained look of awe on her face, as if she didn't quite know whether she was shocked or in pain.

"Was it that bad?" he asked, still leaning over her.

"You didn't kiss me like a friend," she said.

"I've never kissed a friend before. I couldn't know how without having practiced first."

Claire felt an overwhelming urge to cry and wondered desperately why she was having that kind of feeling just because Madison had kissed her.

"So that explains it," she said. "You felt the need to practice."

Laughing softly, he rose to a sitting position. "Are you mad at me?"

No, Claire was angry with herself because she'd wanted him to go on kissing her. She'd wanted to slide her hands across his shoulders, up into his thick, silky hair. She'd wanted to hold him captive against her, kiss him until he was as dazed as she was now.

"No."

"You look as if you are."

She replaced the scowl on her face with a smile. She had to play it light with him. It was the only way. He didn't want to be serious, and she didn't want to be serious, and she couldn't let him know that her heart was feeling otherwise.

"How about now?" she asked.

"That smile looks pretty phony to me," he said, cocking his head to one side and looking closely at her face.

Claire forced her eyes to cling to his and not drift down to his mouth. If she did, she'd be lost.

"That's because I'm actually thinking."

Did she know that he was hanging on her every word? Did she know that he was silently praying she wouldn't turn away from him? He was shaking inside, and it scared the hell out of him.

"What are you thinking?" He tried to keep his voice light, but for some reason his vocal cords were tight and the question came out on a husky note.

As Claire looked into his face, she had the feeling she was at the edge of a bluff, readying herself to jump and knowing there wouldn't be a net below to save her.

"I think we should swim out to the buoys again," she said suddenly.

"Swim out to the buoys!" His voice matched the disbelief on his face.

Claire reached for his hand and tugged. "We're getting hot and lazy sitting here in the sun." And far too serious, she thought. She couldn't let that happen. Because once it did, she'd have to push him away and the joy of being with him would be over.

Madison allowed her to lead him back into the cold water, wishing she would have said more. Something. Anything. Like what? What did you want her to say to you? That she was falling in love with you? he asked himself with sheer frustration. Don't be crazy, Madison! You barely know her and she barely knows you. Besides, you don't want a woman to love you.

He groaned inwardly as they began to swim, wishing his mind would forget Claire and concentrate on the water and the steady rhythm of his strokes, but his mind wouldn't cooperate. It kept saying over and over that he wanted her. Not just sexually, but in another way, too. A way he couldn't understand or explain.

They were swimming side by side now. Every few strokes, Claire would look over and give him a smile.

"Tired?" she called out.

"No. But tomorrow I'll mow the lawn."

She laughed at his winded words, then rolled over and backstroked the rest of the way to the buoys. Madison beat her there. When Claire grabbed onto the cable to rest, he said, "You cheated. You backstroked."

Laughing, she shook the wet hair out of her eyes. "I didn't say you couldn't."

For a moment they were both quiet as they caught their breaths. Finally Claire looked over at him, searching out the blue eyes that had already become dear and familiar to her.

"Madison—"

"Claire—"

They both laughed, then Madison said, "You go first."

"I just wanted to say how nice it is having you with me like this. I don't ever, well, sometimes I forget that there are other things in life besides running a boarding house. Sometimes I even forget that I'm a woman. Thank you for reminding me."

He suddenly reached for her. He couldn't seem to control himself. "Oh God, Claire, don't thank me. It isn't right to thank me."

Claire didn't stop him as one of his hands came up to hold her chin, as his lips opened over hers. The buoyancy of the water brought them together. Claire released her hold on the cable and wrapped her arms around his waist. Their bare legs became tangled and the kiss deepened.

He tasted so good, so male and mysterious that Claire could not bring herself to tear away from him. He was the first man she'd ever really wanted to kiss since her ex-husband and that had been so long ago. She'd never realized how empty and hungry she was until now.

Madison could feel her mouth responding to his and it fueled the want in him. She was warm and soft and so womanly. He wanted more of her, more than he had a right to.

His mouth lifted just enough to allow them both a breath, then he recaptured her lips, this time with his teeth and his tongue.

The erotic feel of his tongue mating with hers had Claire digging her fingers into the muscles of his back. Madison's hand that wasn't holding onto the cable slid down to her bottom and drew her up against him.

Claire could feel his arousal against her and felt the same wanton ache deep inside her. What they were doing was lusty and beautiful and wonderful, but it was also insane and dangerous. She couldn't let it go on!

"Madison! Please—" she whimpered.

"Claire, don't be angry—"

She began to shake her head before he could continue. "I'm not angry. I'm ashamed of myself. I shouldn't want you," she whispered.

"You want me?"

Their faces were only an inch or two apart. Claire slid her hands up to his shoulders, reveling in the feel of his smooth, wet skin beneath her fingers. "Do you want me?" she countered, her eyes gazing straight into his.

Those were two questions that Madison didn't need answered. Claire could surely feel his want, and if she didn't want him she would have already unwound her legs from his and pushed away.

But oh God, she hadn't, he thought. And the feel of her, the idea of possessing her was killing him.

The tip of her tongue reached out and moistened her lips. "You're going to be leaving in a few weeks." She said the words as though they both needed to be reminded of the fact.

Madison nodded soberly. "Yes."

"I won't sleep with you," she said.

Madison suddenly felt sick. "I won't ask you to," he said.

Claire suddenly felt empty. "Well, I guess that settles that," she said.

It settled nothing and they both knew it, but they both needed to pretend that it did. It was easier that way.

Claire continued to hold onto him, wondering why she didn't want to let him go, and wondering how she was going to get through the next few weeks without losing her heart.

Madison lifted his hand and brushed it gently along her cheekbone. "Yes, I guess it will have to," he murmured.

Their eyes met once again and they both wondered why they were lying to each other.

It was well after dark when Claire and Madison arrived home. Everything in the picnic hamper had been eaten, and they were both sunburned and exhausted.

The two of them entered the house to find Liv sitting on the couch. The television was playing, but she didn't appear to be watching it. Claire knew instantly that Liv had been crying. It was that damn Arthur again!

Liv looked up to see Claire and Madison entering the room. Claire was carrying his boots and Madison was carrying the hamper, dirty towels and transistor radio.

Dabbing at her eyes, Liv said, "Oh, you two have been out at the lake?"

Claire set Madison's boots out of the way, then went directly over to Liv and sat down beside her. "Is something wrong, Liv?"

Liv shook her head. "Not really. I'm just angry at Arthur."

Claire put a comforting hand on Liv's shoulder. In the past she'd mostly tried to pass over these tearful bouts. But after spending the day with Madison she was beginning to see Liv's problem with Arthur in a different light. "Liv, I've tried to tell you that men are beasts. When are you going to believe me?"

"Here now! Do I look like a beast?"

Both women glanced up at Madison. He looked the furthest thing from a beast. He looked like a darling. But that's where the danger lies, Claire thought.

"Madison, honey, if Arthur looked like you I'd be beating my head against the wall instead of only shedding a few tears."

Smiling ruefully, Madison sat down on the other side of Liv. "Don't listen to Claire. She doesn't know about men."

"And you do?" Claire asked dryly.

"Of course I do. I'm one," he pointed out arrogantly.

Claire groaned as Liv reached for his hand. He patted it comfortingly.

"So you are, honey," Liv crooned to him.

"What has Arthur done this time? Another woman again?" Claire asked.

"Another woman! Do you mean Arthur is a two-timer?" Madison asked.

Liv sighed painfully. "Not this time. Or at least him and Ruthann didn't have their heads together when I left the club."

Madison threw Claire a questioning glance. Claire shrugged in response. If it wasn't another woman, she didn't know what had happened between the older couple.

"Would you like to tell us about it, Liv?" Madison invited.

His question and his show of concern surprised Claire. Most men his age wouldn't bother themselves to talk with older women, much less be concerned for their feelings.

Liv shook her head, then smiled grimly. "I asked Arthur to marry me."

"You what!" Claire gasped. "Liv! How could you? Where's your pride? Your common sense?"

"Claire, stop badgering the woman," Madison spoke up. "Liv is obviously in love. If she wants to ask a man to marry her, it's her right."

Liv gave him a grateful smile. "I knew you were an understanding man the moment I laid eyes on you. Remember, I told you?"

Madison smiled faintly, his eyes filled with amusement. "Yes. I remember."

Claire groaned. "How do you know she's in love?" she asked Madison. This whole thing was getting too serious as far as she was concerned. She'd taken Liv's infatuation with Arthur with a grain of salt, but it was an entirely different thing now. "You've probably never been in love, and you've obviously never been married. You can't—"

"Claire, it doesn't matter," Liv broke in. "Arthur said no. An emphatic, heartbreaking no." Her voice began to wobble on the last word. Madison patted her shoulder, and Liv looked back up at him with tearful eyes. "He wasn't like you, Madison. He likes the word no."

For some reason Madison felt as phony as hell. Which was crazy because he had nothing to do with Liv's predicament. But he suddenly realized he was like this unknown Arthur. He'd been saying no to women for years. No to love, to marriage, to a family.

"Well, Liv, I wouldn't fret," he said gently. "Arthur was probably just a little stunned by your proposal. He's from an older generation and probably doesn't know that you nineties women go after what you want.''

Claire looked over Liv's head to give him a look. He shrugged as though he didn't know what else to say.

"Understand, my hiney!'' Liv suddenly exclaimed. "That old man understands everything! He's just a money-grubbing old miser, that's what. I'm going to forget him. I really am. He can have that dyed-hair junk dealer!''

Claire had to suddenly hide her smile behind her hand. Liv could get nasty when it came to competition.

Madison asked, "What's this about money? Is money the problem between you?''

Liv crossed her arms over her breasts. Her tears were gone now. She seemed more angry than anything. "Checks. Retirement checks. That's what I live on and that's none of Arthur's damn business. But he thinks it is. He says if he marries me, my checks will be cut off. I guess the old geezer thinks I plan to bleed him dry or something. Madison, I don't want his money!''

"Liv, that may not be what Arthur is thinking,'' Madison pointed out. "Did you ask him?''

Liv shook her head. "By then I was too angry.''

"It certainly sounds like it to me,'' Claire said dryly.

Madison shook his head. "I'd rather think Arthur is afraid that if he marries you, he'll jeopardize your security. He's probably thinking he doesn't have many years left and if he died you'd be left without the money you're receiving now.''

Liv shook her head, but already Claire could see new hope dawning on the woman's face. Oh, Madison, Claire thought, why did you have to go and encourage her? You don't believe in love and marriage anymore than I do.

"Do you really think so, Madison? Oh, you wonderful man!" She quickly kissed Madison on the cheek and then rushed to the front door.

"Where are you going?" Claire practically demanded.

"Back to the club. Arthur and I are going to have a little talk."

"My God, it's nearly ten o'clock and she's going out after a man," Claire groaned as Liv's car started out of the driveway.

Madison looked at her. "And you think there's something wrong with that?"

Sighing, Claire got to her feet. "I just don't want to see her hurt. Liv has become very dear to me. And I . . . know what it's like to be hurt by a man."

Madison stood and Claire tilted back her head as his finger came up beneath her chin. "I think Liv and Arthur will be just fine," he said.

What about us, Madison? she wanted to ask. What's going to happen with us? "I hope so," she murmured.

His eyes searched her face for a moment as though he was making a decision about something.

Finally he said, "I've enjoyed this time with you, Claire. More than you'll ever know."

"I'm glad," she said softly.

She wanted to kiss him so badly that she ached, but she didn't make a move to touch him. She had to forget about touching him, liking him. She had to remember they were going to be "just friends."

Why did this image keep running through his mind? he wondered. The image of carrying Claire up the stairs, into his room and shutting the door and the world behind them. The desire to make the image come true was so strong that he jammed his fists down into his jeans pockets to keep from reaching out for her. How was he ever going to see her as just a friend? He must have been insane to think that idea could ever work.

"Well," he said, feeling suddenly awkward with the moment, "I think I'll go up to bed."

Claire continued to hold his gaze. "Is everything all right?"

His dark brows inched upward. "With what?"

"Your room," she answered. "Do you need more bed linen? More towels?"

A faint smile touched his lips. He needed *her*. Didn't she know that? "No. Everything is fine."

"Well, I'll see you at breakfast then. Good night."

Madison forced himself to step back and away from her. "Yes, good night," he said.

Claire watched him turn and climb the staircase. She longed to go after him. To climb the stairs with him, take him by the hand and lead him into her bedroom. She'd lock the door behind them and make love to him with her body, her heart and her mind. The realization stunned her. She'd believed that all those feelings, those things were gone from her life.

But Madison McCrea had come along and changed all that. How was she ever going to survive once he went back to Texas?

Chapter Eight

A week later Madison stood in what would eventually become the parking lot of the new motel, surveying the work that had been accomplished.

The skeletal framework was up now and tomorrow the men would begin decking the roofs. He was pleased with the way the building would blend aesthetically with the surroundings. That was important to him. He didn't want a building with his signature on it to stand out like a sore thumb, particularly one of this proportion.

Yes, everything was going fine with the job. It was the situation with Claire that was putting a grim look to his face. He didn't know where things between them were heading, or where they would end.

This past week he could feel himself growing closer and closer to her, and he believed that she was growing closer to him. To any other man and woman that would have been good. But not for Claire and Madison, two people who didn't want commitment and marriage.

They were still passing themselves off to each other as friends. And Madison hadn't made the mistake of kissing her again. He was afraid that if he did they would be tempted to forget that they were just friends and then everything would blow up in their faces. It was killing him, though, being with her and not touching her. That day on the lake was always in the back of his mind, taunting him, reminding him of how it could be if they became lovers.

His concentration had practically deserted him, along with his appetite and his usually good humor. He was a man in love and it was making him sick.

"What do you think, Madison? Looks pretty good if you ask me."

Madison glanced over as Ray joined him. "I'm happy with it."

"You sure don't look happy," Ray remarked. "Is something wrong? The past few days you've been off your feed."

Shrugging, Madison slipped the pen he'd been using back into his shirt pocket. "I guess I'm just getting homesick."

The older man looked at him through narrowed eyes. "I've never known you to be homesick before. We stayed on that job in New Mexico for ten weeks and you never went home or even mentioned wanting to go home."

"Ray, there's nothing wrong with me." He turned and began walking back to the trailer. He knew his foreman would follow.

"Why don't you come out with me and the boys to-night and have a few beers?" Ray asked as the two men entered the air-conditioned trailer.

Madison pulled off his cap and raked his fingers through his hair. "No thanks. Claire will be expecting me for supper."

Ray went to pour himself a cup of coffee. Madison tossed his cap aside and sank down in the chair behind his desk.

"She will, huh?"

Madison picked up a pencil and absently tapped the eraser against the ink blotter. "Yes, she will. Besides, I'm building her a doghouse."

"What?"

"I said, I'm building her a—"

"No, no," Ray said after taking a gulp of the thick black brew. "I mean what are you doing building a doghouse?"

Madison peered out the window. He knew it appeared as if he were watching the crew at work, but actually he was seeing Claire, the way she looked as she bustled around the kitchen, the way her skirts swirled around her legs as she moved, the way her teeth flashed against her lips when she smiled, the way her dark hair swung against her back.

"Madison? Do you need a hearing aid?"

"What?"

Ray made an impatient gesture. "The doghouse, remember? Damn, this woman must really have something!"

Madison turned away from the window to toss his foreman a forbidding glance. "Claire is a respectable woman."

The foreman's bushy brows rose in surprise. "You mean you haven't been sleeping with her?"

"No. Not that it's any of your business," Madison said sharply.

Ray took another swig of coffee. "Maybe it's not my business but it tells me a hell of a lot."

"Really?" Madison asked dryly. "Tell me, Mr. Authority, what does it mean?"

Ray ignored Madison's sarcasm. They'd been friends for far too long for anything but open honesty. "It means you're in love with the woman."

Madison's head jerked up. He tossed the pencil to one side. "You're crazy!"

"Hell, Madison, I may be older than you, but I'm still a man. I know about these things. The only time a man doesn't sleep with a woman is when he's in love with her."

"That's the stupidest reasoning I've ever heard!"

A smile began to play around Ray's mouth. "Then why haven't you slept with her?"

Madison's face began to redden. "Because—"

"She doesn't want you near her?"

"No!" It wasn't that, Madison thought. He knew, just as surely as she, that if he pushed the issue they would ultimately wind up making love.

"Then you don't find her attractive enough?"

If he found her any more attractive he was going to explode. "No— I mean yes, I do find her attractive."

"Then she must be married," Ray went on.

"No. She's divorced."

"Maybe you think she's too young?"

Madison let out a frustrated breath. "No. She's older than me."

Ray began to smile smugly. "See what I mean? There's no other reason but love."

"Damn it—" Madison began angrily only to stop when someone banged on the door. He looked at Ray. "You better be glad someone is wanting one of us, because I was getting ready to strangle you, old man."

Ray laughed loudly as he went to answer the door.

Madison's frame of mind hadn't improved much when he left the job site later that evening. As he drove to Claire's house he kept thinking about Ray's theories. Was the man right? It sounded crazy. When two people were in love they slept together. Or did they? He'd slept with women before, but he hadn't loved any of them, he reasoned with himself. Maybe Ray was right. Maybe he did love Claire. But admitting it wouldn't help matters.

She'd told him from the very beginning that she wasn't the marrying kind. And he certainly wasn't a family man. His father and brother were family men. They were good at it. But Madison had never been like his father or his brother, and the few times he'd tried to be like them, it had never worked out. There was no sense in thinking it would this time.

Claire heard Madison the moment he opened the front door. Quickly she threw aside her dish towel and went to meet him.

"Hi," she said.

He smiled and gave her his cap, which she hung on a rack as they progressed to the kitchen. Once there he knew he would find the table on the adjoining porch set for two, delicious smells coming from the range, and the radio playing softly. He'd wash his hands in the sink as though he'd lived there for years and she'd hand him a glass of iced tea. It was routine now.

"Supper's almost ready," she told him as she handed him the frosty glass.

Claire had come to realize over this past week that she'd ceased to think of Madison as a boarder. He was part of her life now, someone she cared about, someone she wanted to be with. Her home was his home. Her heart was his heart. It was almost as if they were husband and wife without the fringe benefits.

"I smell chicken," he said.

She took the lid off the iron skillet and began to fork the golden-brown pieces onto a dish lined with paper towels. "Fried. Not good for our bodies but wonderful for our tastebuds. Are yours working tonight?"

"Is what working?" he asked while busily rolling up the sleeves of his denim shirt. The day had been hot. There was a damp triangle over his chest and on his back. After they ate he'd take off the shirt and Claire would carry it to the washer and wash it for him.

"Your tastebuds. These things, remember?" she asked, sticking her tongue out at him. "Yours didn't seem to be working last night or this morning. Is my cooking boring to you now?"

"Your cooking is delicious. It's just the heat."

Claire looked at him worriedly but said nothing. She didn't want to sound like a harping wife.

He helped her carry the food out to the screened-in porch and she turned on the oscillating fan to stir the muggy air.

"Is Liv out again this evening?" Madison asked as they began to eat.

Claire grimly shook her head. "No. She's gone back to Illinois."

Madison's fork stopped midway to his mouth. "Gone. You mean as in gone for good?"

Claire sighed. "No. Not for good. But something tells me if she doesn't work things out with Arthur she'll be moving back to Illinois permanently. The whole thing is making her miserable."

"She must really love the man," Madison reasoned.

Frowning, Claire chewed a bite of food, then looked over at Madison. "Yes, I should have seen it coming. She'd started talking about how awful it was to be alone and how having family and friends was not like having a soul mate. Maybe if I'd realized what was happening I could have warned her sooner."

"You think a person needs to be warned about falling in love?"

Claire was surprised by his question. "Well, yes, I do. Don't you?"

He shrugged, saying nothing, but his expression was moody. Claire suddenly felt uncomfortable.

"Come to find out about it, Arthur was worried about Liv's security just as you thought," she went on.

"So what's the problem now?"

"He won't give in. Says he doesn't want to be the one to leave her destitute if he should die."

Madison frowned. "I doubt she'd be destitute."

"Well, whatever the case, Liv is going to stay with her daughter a few days. So I guess we'll have the place to ourselves."

Her words brought an array of erotic thoughts, taking Madison's mind completely off the food, but he forced himself to eat anyway. He knew that Claire would be watching and wondering if he didn't eat. He didn't want to have to explain to her that his mind was so consumed with wanting to make love to her that he couldn't think about food or anything else.

Claire stabbed a pea with her fork and absently lifted it to her lips. When she'd watched Liv leave this morning, she'd had all kinds of mixed feelings. With Liv gone, she and Madison would be completely alone. A part of Claire wanted that; the other part didn't think it could deal with the temptation.

After supper Madison went out to his pickup, got his toolbox, shed his shirt, then went to work on the doghouse he was erecting in the backyard. Claire put the dirty dishes in the dishwasher, then joined him, handing him nails and holding boards when needed.

"You don't have to do this now," she told him after they'd worked for more than half an hour. "You're probably tired and would like to rest."

"I'm not tired," he assured her. "And you getting a dog is a good idea. Being a woman alone you need one for protection if nothing else."

Claire smiled faintly. "Liv would have said I needed a man to protect me. You understand me better than she does."

Madison didn't want to think about any man protecting Claire except himself. But what about after he left? he thought dismally. Would some other male boarder move in? Would he take over Madison's room? Would he be sitting at the table with Claire as Madison did, sharing breakfast and supper with her? The whole idea was sickening and he gave the nail head an unnecessarily hard blow.

Looking up at her he asked, "I do? Why? Because I know you're not the marrying kind?"

She looked at him and forced herself to smile, but her heart wasn't in it and it showed in her eyes. Madison didn't smile back.

"That's because you're not the marrying kind, either," she explained.

Madison frowned and said nothing. Claire got the feeling he was angry about something, but she couldn't figure out why. She wasn't all that happy herself, and working next to Madison without his shirt on wasn't helping matters. Her eyes kept drifting off the task at hand to glide over his muscled shoulders and arms, the way his back rippled as he drove the nails into the pine lumber.

Suddenly Claire felt her hold on the board slipping and she reached to get a better grip. At the same time Madison drew down his hammer. Claire's finger accidentally got in the way and she yelled out with pain as it was squashed beneath the hammerhead.

"Oh hell! Oh damn, Claire! Let me see how it looks."

He reached for her hand, but Claire was in such agony all she could do was squeeze the injured finger between her legs and wait for the pain to subside.

"It's...all right," she finally managed to get out between gritted teeth.

"I know it isn't all right," he said, ignoring her words and virtually prying her hand from between her knees. "Your face is white and this finger—"

He held it out where both he and Claire could see the damage. And it was damaged. The blow of the hammer had actually busted open the flesh and blood was beginning to ooze down the side of her arm.

"Come on," he said, tugging her toward the house. "We've got to get this attended to."

"I can do it," she insisted. "You don't have to help."

He was virtually dragging her up the staircase as though he was afraid she was going to bleed to death if she wasn't attended to immediately.

"I'm the one who hurt you," he said quickly. "And it's your right hand."

He led her into his room, then into his bathroom where he made her sit down on the side of the tub while he searched out first aid items.

"It hurts like hell, Madison, but I'm going to live," she told him, as he fumbled with a bottle of peroxide.

"Shut up and come here," he said, drawing her up from the tub and holding her hand over the sink. He poured a good measure of the peroxide over the wound. It foamed and ran everywhere. "Maybe I should take you to the doctor. It might need stitches."

"Don't be silly. It's not that bad. It's mainly bruised and it hasn't been long since I've had a tetanus shot," she tried to reassure him.

"You're bleeding," he said.

"Women do bleed," she told him with a shaky smile.

His hands shook as he wet a washcloth and proceeded to clean her hand and arm and her legs.

"You're being a smart aleck now."

The pain was beginning to ebb to a dull throb. Claire was able to chuckle at him. "I just don't want you to worry."

He pressed on the wound until he was certain the bleeding was going to stop, then proceeded to dress it with ointment and two wide bandages.

Once the tape was smooth and secure on her finger, Madison looked up and into her face. "I'm so sorry, Claire. I didn't mean to hit you."

Claire quickly shook her head. "I know you didn't. It was my own fault. I wasn't watching and I moved my hand. Please don't feel guilty. That would bother me much worse than this finger."

"But I do feel guilty. Is it still hurting?"

"A little. I'll take an aspirin."

He looked horrified. "No! Aspirin is a blood thinner. You'll make it start bleeding again."

"Oh, Madison, that's ridiculous!" She'd never had anyone make such a fuss over her well-being before. It made her feel loved and cared for even though she knew Madison didn't actually love her.

He rummaged through the first aid kit and found a different kind of analgesic, then got her a paper cup full of water. Claire felt him watching her anxiously as she swallowed the two tablets.

"Thank you, Madison. Now quit worrying."

His hand reached out and touched her face as though to reassure himself that the color had come back to her skin.

As his fingers brushed against her cheek, Claire forgot all about her injury. The past few days all she'd been able to think about was him, and now he was touching her. It was more than she could bear.

"Madison—"

She said his name with anguish, telling Madison she was feeling just as frustrated as he. His hand slid down to her neck, then tightened to draw her forward and against him.

Claire knew she should pull away. If they were going to continue to be just friends, they couldn't remain in each other's arms. But as his hands touched her and his lips drew down to hers, a part of her knew she wanted much more from him than friendship.

Madison kissed her hungrily and felt his senses spiraling out of control as she kissed him back with equal fervor. He told his mind to remember all the reasons they should remain apart, but it refused to listen. At the moment nothing mattered to him but holding Claire, kissing Claire.

Lack of air finally forced them to break apart. Claire looked at him with dark, dazed eyes.

"We're not acting like friends," she whispered.

"I want to be more than your friend, Claire. And I know that you want that, too."

Her eyes dropped guiltily to the brown column of his throat. Had she been that easy to read? "Maybe."

In response, his hand reached out and undid the top button on her blouse. Claire felt a weakness in her knees as his knuckles brushed against her breast and his fingers continued their downward path.

One by one she watched the buttons separate from the fabric but still she could not move away from his hand.

Claire felt unable to draw in a breath as he pushed the blouse aside and her breast was bared to his view.

"Claire. My lovely Claire," he murmured.

"Madison, this is insane!" she protested weakly.

"It doesn't feel insane, does it?" he asked softly.

Claire groaned as his head dipped and his lips brushed across of the tops of her breast. Unfamiliar heat swamped her body and her head lolled to one side.

"Madison, I can't do this," she groaned.

"Then don't do anything," he mouthed against her soft skin. "Let me do it all. Let me make love to you, Claire."

His muffled voice was just as erotic as his touch. Her fingers thrust into his dark hair, but instead of pushing his head away, she held him to her, her hardened nipples aching for his mouth to find them.

When it did, she moaned aloud, shocked at the unbidden desire surging through her body. She wanted him with a ferocity she'd never felt before. She felt weak with relief when he stooped to pick her up and carry her out to his bed.

Before Madison laid her down, he peeled away her blouse and tossed it to the foot of the bed. The bedspread felt cool against Claire's back and she knew it was because her skin was already overheated.

Madison kneeled over her and their eyes met for long searching moments. Claire saw hunger in his. That and something else. Was it love? Hope? Vulnerability?

Claire's eyes were dark, cloudy, full of tenderness and desire. Madison wanted to worship every inch of her, wanted to feel her soft body yield to his over and over again.

"Do you know how much I want you, Claire? How much I've wanted you these past days?"

Claire did know. She'd wanted him just as badly and she'd fought it long and hard. But now, for the moment, she'd quit fighting. "Yes, I do," she said softly.

Her answer brought a groan from deep within his throat. His head lowered, his eyes closed. Claire reached up to encircle his neck with her arms. Then her eyes closed, too, and their lips found each other.

Madison's tongue plundered the dark recesses of her mouth. In turn. Claire gently nipped his lower lip, his chin, his jaw and earlobe.

He flattened his chest against her breast and relished the sensation of having her against him. Claire moved restlessly beneath him, wanting him, needing him.

Madison clutched her to him as a host of feelings began to overtake him. There was a fierce ache inside him to show her how much he cared, to show her that he was unlike the man who'd hurt her in the past. He was a man who could love her, never hurt her. And the realization of his thoughts paralyzed him.

The moment he grew still Claire's mind edged away from him and back to reality. She couldn't let him make love to her, she thought desperately. If she did there would be no turning back. She would be bound to him by heart and body. Whereas he would view the whole thing as an affair. A thing that would be over once his job was over. She'd had her heart and her self-esteem shattered once, she couldn't let it happen again.

They drew apart at the same time, as if they both understood that something had gone awry. Claire had a wounded look on her face. Madison appeared dazed.

With slow, jerky movements, Claire reached for her blouse and clutched it to her breast.

"I'm . . . sorry, Madison," she whispered sadly. "I can't let this happen between us."

Madison sucked in a deep breath and raked his fingers through his dark tousled hair. "I know."

She glanced at his face and saw anguish on it. "You know?"

He nodded while turning his back to her and lifting his face toward the ceiling. Claire got the impression that he was hurting just as badly as she was.

"Friends don't make love," he said as though that explained everything.

Claire suddenly felt tears sting her eyes and spill onto her cheeks. "We're not friends."

"Yes, we are," he said gruffly. "We have to be. Otherwise—"

He didn't finish. Claire sniffed miserably and wiped her eyes. Madison turned and groaned aloud at the sight of Claire in tears.

"You think I'll be like your ex-husband, don't you? You think I'll hurt you?"

She lifted her head and looked at him calmly. "Not in the same way. He liked wine and women, and he liked to say that I wasn't woman enough for any man. Maybe that's true but—"

"That's rubbish," he broke in.

Pain ebbed in her chest. "I don't want to take the chance of finding that out with you. Besides," she went on, dropping her eyes away from his, "I can't give you a part of me, knowing you'll be leaving in a few weeks, and knowing I'd never get that part of me back."

Strangely, Madison knew exactly what she was trying to say. But he didn't know how to ease her pain, or his pain, or make any of it better. He only knew there was a frustration inside him such as he'd never known. "Claire, I—"

The telephone beside the bed began to ring loudly, cutting off whatever he'd been about to say. They both stared at it as if they'd forgotten there was a world going on around them.

"Would you get that?" she asked him. "I don't want to talk now."

He reached over to the nightstand and lifted the receiver. "Hello. Yes, this is Madison," he spoke.

Long moments passed without him saying anything. Curious, Claire looked over her shoulder and unexpectedly found a stricken look on his face. It was obvious something was very wrong.

"Yes, I'll be there as quickly as I can," he finally said. "Tonight, if possible. Yes, tell him I'll be there one way or the other."

Claire saw that his face was white as he replaced the phone back on its cradle. "What is it? What's the matter?"

"My brother," he said tightly.

Claire didn't ask more. Instead she waited for him to collect himself. Her gaze moved along with him as he headed to the closet.

"He's been in an accident," Madison went on. "A storm hit an offshore rig. Mitch was on it."

"I'm so sorry." Claire was suddenly afraid for Madison's sake. "How badly was he injured?"

Madison's features were grim as he tossed the suitcase down on the end of the bed. "Right now he's listed as critical. They've airlifted him to Houston."

Claire forced herself into action. Obviously he needed to leave quickly. At least she could help him gather his things. Quickly she pulled on her blouse and slipped off the bed.

"I can help you pack. Let me have your shaving bag and I'll get your razor and things." She reached for the small leather bag lying beside his suitcase.

Madison's hand closed around her wrist, bringing Claire's eyes up to his face.

"I hate to leave you like this, Claire."

There was desperation in his voice and on his face. Claire wasn't sure if it was because of his leaving or because his brother's life was in danger. Either way, Claire hated for him to leave now. Especially after what had just happened between them.

"Your family needs you."

He dropped her hand and moved away. "A part of them," he said tightly.

Claire glanced at him. The urge to ask him what he meant by the statement was strong, but she pushed it aside and turned her attention back on the packing. Now was not the time for questions. He had to go.

Fifteen minutes later Claire stood waiting in the living room while Madison gave last-minute instructions over the telephone to his foreman.

When he hung up, Claire reached for one of his smaller cases and left the other two larger ones for him to carry out to his pickup.

"You won't give my room to someone else, will you?" he asked as she pitched one of the suitcases onto the front seat.

Claire summoned a smile to her face as he turned to her. "Of course not. We have a contract, remember?"

A faint smile touched his lips. "I'll be back as soon as Mitch is out of danger—whenever that will be."

She kept waiting for him to say he would call or write. When he didn't she felt even more dejected.

"I'll be . . . looking for you," she said, her voice unusually husky.

Their eyes caught and held and Claire thought how strange it was that for those few minutes in each other's arms they'd communicated as if they'd always known how. But now she was at a loss to tell him how she was feeling, and from the look of frustration on his face, he was, too.

"Goodbye, Claire. Take care."

She nodded, her throat growing thick, making it impossible to get a word out.

Swiftly he bent his head and kissed her softly on the lips. The urge to cling to him was strong and she realized that she'd grown far more attached to Madison than she'd ever intended to let herself be.

He turned away from her, climbed into the truck and started the engine. Claire stepped back and gave him a little wave. The next thing she knew she was watching the back end of his truck disappear from sight.

Chapter Nine

Five days later, Claire was in the yard, watering the flowers and shrubs when the telephone rang. Quickly, she turned off the hose and rushed inside to snatch up the receiver.

"Hello," she answered in a breathless voice.

"Hello, sweetie. How are you?"

At the sound of Liv's voice, Claire's shoulders slumped. Since Madison had gone, she'd remained close to the phone, hoping that he would call. But so far she'd heard nothing.

"Liv! I'm glad you called. How are things going up there?"

"It's really been boring up here, Claire," she said with a sigh. "I miss all my friends at the club. And of course I miss you. How are you and Madison getting on? Like a house on fire I'll bet," Liv added with a knowing giggle.

Claire's already low spirits sunk even lower. "Madison isn't here, Liv. His brother was in a bad accident and he left five days ago to be with his family."

"Oh, I'm sorry to hear that. How's his brother doing now?"

Claire sank into a nearby stuffed armchair. "I don't know, Liv," she said, unaware of the desperation in her voice. "I haven't heard a word from Madison. I really don't know what's happened with him or his family."

"Hmm, that surprises me. Didn't you tell him to call or drop you a line?"

"Er, no, I didn't. But I thought that—"

"Claire! The poor boy thinks you're not interested. That's why he hasn't bothered to contact you."

"You're wrong, Liv. I did let him know that I...was interested. But he behaved like your Arthur and ran backward."

Liv clucked with disapproval. "Men can be real pains in the you-know-what, Claire. But if you try hard enough you can make him run to you."

"How can you say that so confidently? You gave up on Arthur and ran away to Illinois."

Liv giggled. "Oh no, Claire, I didn't run away. I'm just using a little strategy on the old goat. He'll come around and so will Madison."

"Liv, it's pretty obvious that Madison isn't serious about me. It's been five days without a word from him. I know he's in a family crisis, but surely he could spare two or three minutes on the telephone."

Liv's laughter tinkled in Claire's ear. "For a woman who vowed to never fall in love, you sure sound smitten now."

Claire felt her face burning and was glad the older woman wasn't there to see it. "Madison is a renter," she explained defensively.

"And he'll be back," Liv calmly assured. "After all, he's building a motel in town."

Yes, he would be back eventually, Claire thought. But the present was the thing that was bothering her. The fact that he hadn't called or written spoke for itself, and it was something she found hard to face. For Madison those moments in each other's arms had only been an expression of desire, whereas she'd felt much more than just wanting.

"I don't want to talk about Madison anymore, Liv. So how are things going for you? Have you heard from Arthur?"

The older woman snorted. "Oh yes. He called, wanting me to come home to Eureka Springs. I told him there was no future there for me."

"And what did he have to say about that?" Claire asked.

"He said people our age don't have futures, we only have one day at a time."

"I'm sorry, Liv. It sounds as though Arthur is having trouble coming to terms with things. But don't give up. Maybe he'll come around."

"See what Madison has done for you, Claire?" Liv said smugly. "A few days ago you were telling me to forget Arthur and that all men were beasts," she reminded.

Claire sighed, knowing Liv was right. It seemed impossible that Madison had changed her way of thinking in such a short time. But he had. "Well, I can see that you truly love Arthur. And . . . and I want you to be happy.''

"Actually," Liv said, her voice lowering to nearly a whisper, "my daughter thinks I'm crazy for wanting to marry again. But I gave her that old bit about walking in someone else's shoes before giving judgment. She hasn't been so quick to open her mouth now," she added smugly.

Claire hated to think that Liv was having trouble from both Arthur and her daughter. "Come back home, Liv. You can stand your ground here with Arthur as well as up there. The house is like a tomb without you."

Liv laughed. "I suppose it is. But you're missing Madison, not me. And I'm telling you, Claire, if you feel something deep for the man, don't push it or him aside. Life's too precious to spend it alone."

Claire's throat was suddenly thick as thoughts of Madison rose in her mind. She was forced to swallow before she could respond. "I'll remember, Liv."

"I've got to go now, sweetie. My daughter's planned a big day for me. Two neighbors are coming over for penny-ante poker and lemonade. But I'm slipping off to the tennis court later," she whispered sassily.

Claire laughed softly, glad to hear Liv wasn't letting anything get to her. "Bye, Liv. Let me hear from you soon."

"I will. Goodbye now."

Claire hung up and as usual felt as if she'd been sucked up in a whirlwind after talking to Liv. For a moment she simply sat there, thinking about the older woman and all she'd said.

In all honesty she missed Madison terribly. Each time the phone had rung these past days, her heart had leapt in her throat from her thinking it might be him. She didn't want to miss him. She didn't want to care about him. But she did, and she was afraid it was too late to change her feelings now.

Two days later was Sunday night and Claire had been in bed nearly an hour when she heard a faint knock on the front door downstairs.

After tying a thin wrapper over her nightgown, she hurried down the staircase to answer it. "Who is it?" she called out, while switching on the porch light. She'd never been afraid of burglars, but she never foolishly opened her door to anyone at night.

"It's me, Claire. Madison."

Claire's heart was suddenly pounding in her chest as she fumbled with the latch. Finally, she was swinging the door wide to see him standing in front of her. His suitcases were sitting on the porch just behind him.

"Hello," she said, smiling, her voice warm and husky. She motioned him into the house as she moved aside to allow him entrance. "Do you need help with your bags?"

He reached behind him and handed her the small travelling bag she'd helped him pack a week ago. "I can get these two," he told her.

Claire waited until he was inside, then shut and locked the door behind him. Turning back, she expected him to be there, but to her amazement he was already climbing the stairs.

Claire followed, trying to push away her disappointment. She'd expected him to greet her more warmly, perhaps even pull her into his arms and kiss her. Had these past days he'd spent away from her erased everything between them? she wondered.

"I was beginning to worry about you, Madison," she said, entering his room to find him tossing his suitcases onto the bed. "How's your brother?"

Without looking her way he said, "He was in pretty bad shape when I got there. But he's better now."

Claire went on into the room and placed the bag she was carrying along with the others. "I'm glad to hear he's better. Is he still in the hospital?"

He finally looked up at her and a brief smile touched his mouth. Claire's heart contracted. He looked so terribly exhausted and the sparkle in his blue eyes she'd grown so used to seeing was nowhere to be found. He looked like a man who'd faced defeat. But that didn't make sense. He'd just told her his brother was better.

"I'm afraid he'll be there for some time. His back was broken and required twelve hours of surgery. For a while they weren't sure if he would be paralyzed."

"Oh Madison, how horrible! Will he recover fully?" She was almost afraid to ask. Madison's expression was so guarded she got the feeling he didn't want to discuss any of it with her. The idea hurt more than it should have.

"Yes, thank God. The recovery will be slow, but he will eventually get back to normal."

She let out a breath of relief. "That's wonderful," she said, then unable to stop herself, she went to him and laid her hand on his arm. "Would you like coffee?" she asked softly. "You must be exhausted."

Madison looked down at her sweet, beautiful face and felt his insides turn over. He'd actually been dreading seeing Claire again. He'd known how much she would still affect him, how much he would still want her.

"Thanks, coffee would be nice."

She smiled again and his eyes were drawn to her mouth. While he was away, that smile had stayed in his memory like a familiar melody he couldn't shake.

"It won't take a minute," she promised, turning and hurrying out of the room.

His eyes followed her and he groaned inwardly. This past week he'd had to face up to many things, one of them being Claire and where she fit into his life. He thought he'd made a decision about it, but now, seeing Claire again, he felt that decision splintering in all directions.

A few minutes later on the screened-in porch, she served Madison the coffee and a bowl of apple cobbler.

"Is Liv still in Illinois?" he asked as Claire took a seat to the left of him.

Claire nodded. "She called a couple of days ago. I tried to get her to come home, but apparently she's not ready to face Arthur."

Madison looked over at her. The silky wrapper she was wearing was a deep green color that matched the green in her hazel eyes. Her curves gave the flimsy material a shape that ignited a flame inside him. He'd never known he could miss a woman so much until he'd been separated from Claire. His mind had gone over and over every subtle line of her face, every lush curve of her body. Now they were alone and he was aching to make love to her.

"I thought she'd be back by now," he said, returning his gaze to his food.

It almost sounded as if he wished Liv were back so there would be no possibility of their repeating that scene in his bedroom. Claire fiddled with the handle on her coffee mug. It would probably be better if Liv was back, she thought dismally. "So did I."

He didn't say anything and Claire watched him eat, feeling a tension fill the silent room. The night was very warm and beyond the porch, insects buzzed and sang. In the far distance, between the dappled shadows of maple branches, a full moon could be seen rising over the mountains. Claire wondered how they would have been spending this night if he'd never gone to Houston. In his bed? In each other's arms?

The questions left her aching and confused. Finally she pulled her eyes away from him and focused them on her cup.

Madison glanced at Claire's hands and noticed the finger he'd smashed with the hammer had a new bandage. "How's your finger?"

Heat flooded through Claire as she was reminded of that day and how badly she'd wanted him to make love to her. No doubt he was remembering it, too. "It's fine."

Long moments passed in awkward silence. Finally Claire said, "I suppose you stayed with your family while you were in Houston."

"With my sister-in-law, Raylene," he spoke. "She and Mitch have two young children. She thought it would help them to have their Uncle Madison around while their father was in the hospital."

There was a faint mocking twist on his mouth when he finished speaking. Claire wondered what had put it there. "I'm sure it did. But you sound doubtful. Why? I thought you liked children?"

Finished with the cobbler, he pushed the bowl away and reached for his coffee. "I do like children, but I'm no daddy."

"I hope not," she said teasingly, hoping to bring him out of his down mood.

The frown on his face suddenly vanished and he smiled wanly at her. He'd tried to forget how wonderful it felt to be with her, but he'd found that was like trying to forget the beauty of a summer sunrise.

"I've missed you, Claire."

"What does that mean?" she asked softly, an earnest light filling her eyes.

His expression became guarded. "Just what I said," he whispered. "I missed you."

It wasn't exactly what she wanted to hear, but it was enough. Without considering the consequences, she rose from the chair and slipped onto his lap. "Oh, Madison," she groaned, curling her arms around his neck. "I've missed you, too. Terribly."

Her actions took him by surprise, but the feel of her soft body pressing into his quickly overrode everything. His arms moved around her waist, instinctively drawing her to him.

"Oh, Claire. You shouldn't be here like this," he murmured against her dark hair.

She pushed away from him so she could look into his eyes. "I probably shouldn't," she said in sad agreement. Her hands came up and gently touched his face. "You didn't even bother to call me. And I know you don't want commitment, or marriage, but . . . damn it, Madison, you look terrible and—"

Madison suddenly couldn't bear it any longer. One hand came up and cupped the back of her head, drawing her face against his. "And I came back, telling myself I wasn't going to let this happen again. But I still want you," he muttered gruffly.

"Madison—"

The rest was cut off as his mouth took hers with a hunger that stole her breath away. As his lips savored the familiar taste of hers, his hands moved against her warm body, caressing, searching until his fingers slipped beneath the silk and curved around a firm breast.

A sharp ache rushed through Claire, so sweet and powerful that for a moment she forgot where they were. She was totally lost to the passion in his kiss, the urgency of his hands against her. She'd missed him, yearned for him, and even more she'd realized that her life without him would be gray. To be in his arms like this was something she could hardly refuse herself.

It was Madison who tore his mouth away and buried his face in the side of Claire's neck. He drew in ragged breaths and tried to fight off the desire drugging his mind.

"I told myself I'd be better off if I didn't come back," he said hoarsely. "But here I am."

Here he was, but it wasn't where he wanted to be. The words were as plain as if he'd spoken them and they cut Claire deeply. Quickly, she pushed out of his arms and moved to the opposite side of the porch. "Maybe I would have been better off if you hadn't come back," she said in a low, broken voice, "but here

I am falling all over you anyway. I guess it must be true about older women losing their heads over younger men."

She'd turned her back on him as she spoke and Madison watched her shoulders rise and fall as she drew in deep breaths. Everything inside him was begging to go to her and take her in his arms again. But he knew if he touched her right now, he wouldn't be able to control himself.

"Do you want me to leave?"

His unexpected question had her whirling around to stare at him. It would probably be better for both of them if she said yes, she thought. But it would all be over if she did, and she didn't want that, no matter what kind of pain his staying might bring.

"No. I don't want you to leave. After all, we have a contract, and I always honor my contracts," she said softly, then turned and left the room.

Madison wasn't aware he'd been holding his breath until Claire was out of sight, then the air whooshed out of him. The pain on her face as she'd walked out tore him to pieces. Madison didn't want to hurt her, but he could already see that if he kept his distance from her it was going to hurt both of them.

Biting back a curse, he raked his fingers through his hair, then went to pour himself another cup of coffee. He'd stay downstairs until he was certain Claire was behind her own bedroom door and completely out of sight. He didn't want to take the chance of running into her again. Desire was still clouding his common sense, making him wonder how he was ever going to get through these next few weeks without ruining both their lives.

* * *

Upstairs Claire lay rigidly on the bed, her eyes staring unseeingly out the window. Madison's return had been nothing like she'd expected or hoped for. It had made her see that she'd been a fool to read anything into that last day they'd spent together. But she couldn't get it—or him—out of her mind.

She understood that he'd been through a frightening experience with his brother and that in itself had probably left him feeling down. But his brother was on the road to recovery now.

While he'd been gone Claire had thought and hoped that when he returned they could talk about the feelings between them. And maybe, just maybe, he would come around to seeing he needed her as much as she needed him. But after tonight it was obvious he was trying to put distance between them. Now it was up to her to find out exactly why.

At breakfast the next morning Claire bustled around the kitchen, humming along with the radio as if nothing was amiss. Because it really wasn't all that amiss, she tried to assure herself as she mixed waffle batter.

She'd known before Madison left for Houston that he didn't want marriage or commitments. Neither had she. But being without him for seven long days had shown her just how much she really cared about him. She'd changed her mind. Now she knew she had to change his.

Madison entered the kitchen to see Claire at the cabinets, her back to him. The radio was tuned to the soft rock station she always listened to, and the smell of bacon and rich coffee permeated the air. She was wearing a red sundress cut halter style. The circle skirt swished gently against her shapely calves as she worked a wire whisk through the batter.

Everything was the same as he remembered and though he'd told himself that routine bored him, it was food for his heart to see Claire like this again.

"Good morning," he said, walking into the room.

She looked over her shoulder and smiled at him. He looked better this morning. Most of the fatigue was gone from his face, telling her he must have slept. She longed to go to him and touch him in some way, but his look didn't invite it. "Good morning. I hope you're hungry, I'm making waffles," she told him.

He reached for a cup and walked over to the coffeemaker. "Yes, I am. This past week has been so hectic my meals haven't been very regular."

It showed, Claire thought. He looked thinner, but she didn't say so. "I imagine you're anxious to get back on the job. Did they make much progress without you?"

He shrugged and went to take a seat at the pine table. "Ray called me every day. Things have been running pretty smoothly, or so he says. If the truth were known, he could probably build the thing without me."

The words were so unlike the Madison she knew that for a moment she forgot spreading the batter on the hot waffle iron and merely stared at him. "I really doubt that, Madison. It is your company, after all."

He pulled his eyes away from her and down to the coffee cup in his hand. Frustrated, Claire went back to filling the waffle iron.

"What have you been doing while I was away?" he finally asked.

Missing you, thinking about you, Claire silently answered. "Not much," she said aloud. "Just keeping busy around the house. I did a little shopping and went to the library. We had severe thunderstorms one night and my neighbors called me over to go to the cellar with them. Yesterday I worked on income tax records."

She turned around to face him while the waffle finished cooking. "I suppose you spent most of your week sitting in the hospital with your brother?"

He gave one short nod. "Mostly."

Claire's eyes traveled over him while wondering why he was being so evasive. "Your parents were probably very glad to see you. Especially at such a trying time."

A frown crossed his face. Claire didn't know if it was because she was irritating him with her questions or because of something that went on down in Houston.

"Mother was glad to see me," he said.

Claire was forced to turn and retrieve the waffle before it burned. She carried it over to his waiting plate. "And what about your dad?" she persisted.

His face was suddenly dark. "If you don't mind, Claire, I'd really like to change the subject."

Claire didn't want to change the subject, but she would this time because it was his first morning home and she didn't want to start the day arguing with him. Still, it hurt to know he didn't want to share himself with her.

She went back to the counter to finish cooking. Behind her Madison's expression was moody as he spread butter and poured syrup over his waffle.

He didn't want to shut her out, but he couldn't bring himself to tell her exactly how things had gone in Houston. In fact, he'd hoped that once he was back in

Arkansas he could put the whole incident out of his mind. But so far it had been impossible.

When Claire joined him at the table, he lifted his eyes to her. Her expression was quiet and serene. It affected him more than if she'd been angry with him and he wondered if she'd decided there could be nothing between them. She'd professed to having sworn off men, but Madison had tasted the passion in her kiss. Maybe now that he'd awakened it, she would turn her attention to someone else. The idea put a tight knot in his stomach.

"I thought maybe you'd gone on a date with the boor," he tried to say as casually as he could.

Claire looked at him and laughed as though she found his suggestion outrageous. "Not hardly. Saul would never make the mistake of asking me out again. I made it clear to him how I felt."

Madison cursed himself for being so relieved. After a couple of bites of waffle, he said, "You could have changed your mind about things."

She looked up at him and smiled, though the expression in her eyes was somber. "I have, Madison."

His fork stopped midway to his mouth as his eyes narrowed on her face. "About what?" he asked quietly.

She held his gaze even though her heart was pounding. "About us."

Chapter Ten

"About us?" he repeated warily.

"From your attitude I take it you believe there is no us. But I do," she said quietly.

"Claire," he began with a weary shake of his head. "Last week when I—when we—if we'd made love, it would have been a big mistake."

His words broke her calm and she glared at him. "Is that what you've told women in the past?"

He muttered something under his breath and dropped his fork back to the table. "You're not like other women, Claire."

"I'm so thankful for small favors," she said sarcastically.

"You know what I mean," he retorted.

Claire glanced down at her plate and drew in a ragged breath. "I suppose you think all the time we've spent together is a mistake," she said, her voice losing most of its sting.

"No, I— hell, Claire, we've been through this before. You're not the marrying kind. I'm not the marrying kind. It's very simple as I see it. The best thing we can do is just be friends and let it go at that."

Claire's head jerked up and she stared at him, completely dumbfounded. She could see nothing simple about any of it, and for him to say so infuriated her. "And that would make you happy?"

Madison suddenly shoved his plate away and rose to his feet. "Happy? What's happy?" he bit out. "You tried being married before, Claire, were you happy then? Was your mother happy?"

Claire jumped to her feet. "You presumptuous ass! I'm not asking you to walk down the aisle this afternoon. I'm not even asking you to jump into bed with me this afternoon."

"Then what are you asking?"

She waved her hand in a gesture of frustration. "To care, Madison. To care enough not to turn your back on us. But I can see that's asking too much of you." She wheeled away from him and started out of the room.

"Claire, where are you going?" he demanded.

"It doesn't matter," she called back to him, as she disappeared out the door.

Madison quickly followed, catching up to her just as she was entering her small office. He stepped through the door and she whirled around, her face angry.

"Your breakfast is getting cold," he said.

Her heart was aching and he was talking about eating. She wanted to throw something at him! "I've had all I want," she said crisply.

His thumbs looped over the waistband of his jeans as he stood in the middle of the small room, his eyes dark and searching as they roamed her face. "Somehow I get the feeling you're talking about me instead of breakfast."

Tears were suddenly choking Claire. She didn't want to fight with him. She wanted them to be together, loving each other, making each other happy. And they could make each other happy, she knew, if he would only take the chance.

"If that were the case I'd have thrown you out last night." Her chin lifted a fraction as she fought the moisture swimming in her eyes. "But I'm not going to let you off the hook that easily, Madison."

A part of Madison didn't want to be let off the hook, but another part wanted to turn as far as he could from her and the feelings she evoked in him. "Maybe I want to leave," he said, the confidence of her statement making him throw up any kind of barrier against her.

"Do you?" she asked softly.

Damn it, they both knew he didn't. Why was she doing this to him? he wondered. "In spite of my better judgment, no," he told her.

Claire could see the anguish on his face and wanted more than anything to take it away. She moved forward until she was standing next to him, then reached down for his hand and pressed both of hers around it.

"I don't want you to leave, Madison. We...the time we've spent together has been so good," she said in a softly yearning voice. "And while you were gone I realized that I don't want that to end. But last night you were so indifferent, and now—"

Suddenly his hand reached out and touched her face. His eyes closed and his throat worked as he swallowed.

"Oh, Claire, don't you understand that I have to be indifferent with you?"

"Why?" she whispered desperately.

His eyes opened and looked down into hers. "Because I can't keep my senses around you."

"And caring about me would mean losing your senses?" she asked, not bothering to hide the hurt in her voice.

He shook his head. "Look, Claire, you said you've been doing a lot of thinking, well, so have I. And while I was in Houston I decided I'm just not cut out for any kind of lasting relationship."

Claire's instinct told her to be angry with him, but she knew that wouldn't get them anywhere. Besides, she had the feeling that the first part of what he'd said was more important than the last. Something or someone in Houston had changed him. But for now she wasn't going to press him about it.

Forcing a smile on her face, she drew his hand to the place between her breasts. "Perhaps you are right, Madison. Maybe we should just be friends. I've spent twelve years alone. I can probably spend the next twelve just as easily without a man."

A perplexed look came over his face, and doing her best to ignore it, Claire released his hand and walked over to her desk.

Amazed, Madison watched her take a seat and reach for a stack of papers. "You mean you agree?" he asked.

Without looking at him, she shrugged and began to write across the bottom of a ledger sheet. "Of course. I'd never beg any man to care about me."

Just like she'd have to, Madison thought angrily. There would be a line of men at her door if she were to make it known she was available for dating. "Claire! You just asked me to care!"

She lifted her face, surprised that she was able to come up with a bland expression. "So I did," she said offhandedly. "Just put it down to the fact that I'm a middle-aged divorcée. You younger men can make us say anything."

She was playing with him and it was all Madison could do not to go around the desk and kiss the indifference off her face. Instead he muttered an oath, then turned and left the room.

"Goodbye, Madison. See you at supper," she called sweetly after him.

Madison was relieved to see the construction on the motel had been progressing while he'd been gone. Some of the rafters were being raised and as he parked his truck he could see Ray up on a scaffold shouting an order to Fred, who was working ten feet below him with a power saw.

It was good to get back to work, he thought, slapping on his hard hat and climbing out of the truck. The thunderstorms Claire had mentioned were evident in the puddles of water on the ground. Madison skirted around the bigger ones but his boots were still caked with mud by the time he reached the men.

Ray spotted Madison first and shouted a greeting. After that the whole crew came over to him with hellos and questions about his brother's health. For a while work came to a standstill, but it lifted Madison's spirits to know there were those who believed in him and looked to him both as a friend and a man who knew his job. Houston had dragged him down. He hated to admit it, but it had, and he knew he'd never go back. It wasn't worth it. Family just wasn't worth it.

Later that morning Ray followed Madison into the little office for a cup of coffee and an update on the work progress.

After hanging his hard hat on a peg, Madison poured himself a cup of coffee and took a seat at the messy desk. Ray followed, taking his cup to a worn couch jammed into one end of the room.

"It's good to have you back," the foreman said. "It's been hell around here with you gone."

Madison lifted his eyes from the blueprints in front of him to look at Ray. "You said things had been going fine."

Ray mouthed a curse word that Madison had never uttered in his life. "That was only to keep you from worrying. You had enough on your mind with your brother."

Madison sipped the bitter brew from his cup and tried not to grimace. It tasted awful after Claire's smooth coffee.

"So what was the trouble?" Madison asked.

"I had hell with the building inspector over the wiring."

Madison made a disgusted sound. "We're using one of the highest graded materials made. What was the problem?"

Ray shrugged. "Something about the way the men had worked it between the firewalls. Anyway, we finally got it settled. Then two of the men got drunk one night and came to work the next morning only half sober."

Madison's expression visibly hardened. "I hope you fired them."

Ray shook his head. "No, but I threatened them within an inch of their lives."

Madison leaned back in his chair, his hard gaze leveled on the foreman. "Do you understand what it would do to this company if someone had an accident while under the influence of alcohol?"

Ray nodded. "I do. But they won't do it again. I can promise you that."

"You're too damn softhearted, Ray."

The big foreman grinned. "Look who's talking. You hired Leo only two weeks after he'd gotten out of the penitentiary."

Madison shook his head. "I felt he needed a chance to prove himself. And I've never regretted it."

Ray blew on his coffee as he closely regarded Madison. "Have you forgotten how to eat? You look like you've skipped a few meals since you've been in Houston."

Madison shrugged and dropped his eyes back to the blueprints. "The food in the hospital cafeteria wasn't all that wonderful."

Ray grunted with amusement. "Not greasy enough for you, eh?"

"Something like that."

"Or maybe you've been missing Claire?"

Madison looked at Ray, surprised that the older man had remembered her name. Had Madison talked that much about her? he wondered. "She has nothing to do with my eating habits." He reached for a pencil, then picked up one of the orders lying in front of him. "Now, are you ready to get to work?"

"Oh, you don't want to talk about Claire?"

He turned a hard glare on Ray, but the foreman merely grinned. "I just wondered how you fared without her this past week."

"I fared fine. Why shouldn't I?"

"I don't know. You tell me," Ray said casually. "Before you left you wouldn't spend a night out with us boys. You kept saying Claire would be waiting for you with . . . supper."

And Madison had wanted to spend his every spare minute with her. He still did. But to do so would only be asking for trouble. Claire was already asking more from him. Things that he just wasn't ready to give. "Well, all that's changed now," he spoke before he had a chance to stop himself. "So count me in tonight."

Suddenly Ray was on the edge of his seat. "You're going out with us boys tonight?"

"That's what I said," Madison answered sharply.

Ray opened his mouth to say something else, then at the last minute decided to keep it to himself. His eyes narrowed with speculation on the younger man. "That's good. It'll be just like old times, won't it?"

"Just like old times," Madison repeated dourly.

* * *

Claire was in the bathtub when she heard Madison climb the stairs and enter his room. It was well past ten and she'd long ago given up on his returning for supper.

As she stepped out of the tub, she wondered if something had come up to keep him at work, or if he'd just stayed out to avoid her. Probably the latter, she thought dismally, trying to push the ache out of her heart. These past few days she'd desperately wished her mother were alive.

It was true the woman had made a bad choice as far as men were concerned, but it had seemed so long since Claire had felt a loving hand on her shoulder, particularly that of her mother.

Thinking about it now, Claire had really had no loved ones in her life since her aunt had died. Madison had come along and shown her that. It was ironic really. He'd shown her how to love again, but he still couldn't give love himself.

Sometime later she slipped out of her bedroom and past Madison's door. There was a slit of light coming from under it, and she could hear the shower running. More than likely he was getting ready for bed.

Quietly, she went down to the kitchen. After brewing herself a pot of tea, she carried it and the fixings on a tray back to the living room and switched on the television, careful to keep the volume low.

A few minutes later, Madison descended the stairs and found Claire curled up on one end of the couch, sipping tea and watching a late night talk show. He hadn't expected her to be up and the sight of her stopped him in his tracks.

Claire turned her head to see him hovering on the bottom step and said, "I'm only watching TV. You won't disturb me if you're going to the kitchen."

Reluctantly he stepped into the room. Other than the television, there was only one dim light burning at the end of the couch. It cast a soft glow over Claire and he swallowed convulsively at the sight of her.

"I thought you were in bed," he said.

She leaned forward and placed her cup and saucer on the coffee table. "No. Not yet. I hope the television wasn't disturbing you."

The flowered garment she was wearing was whisper thin, gossamer-like as it floated against the thrust of her breasts. Madison's eyes followed its movement as he imagined what it would be like to go to her and pull her into his arms, slip his hands beneath that fabric and touch her soft, heated flesh.

"No," he said, his erotic thoughts making his voice a bit husky. "I didn't hear it at all."

She looked up at him. "I'm sorry you had to work late. I saved something from supper for you. It's in the microwave."

Why did she have to be so damn nice? he wondered. It made him feel even more miserable. "I've already eaten. I went out with some of the crew."

So he had stayed out to avoid her, she thought sickly. "No problem. It was only a rib eye. The crows will enjoy it tomorrow." She picked up the teapot and refilled the cup. Without glancing his way, she added sugar, stirring it slowly and methodically.

"Sorry," he muttered. "I'll reimburse you for it."

Carefully cradling her cup with both hands, Claire leaned back against the cushions of the couch. "Your rent paid for it,'' she said far more casually than she felt. Did the damn man think she cared only about the money? she wondered. Didn't he know she'd sat for hours waiting and watching for him? Or did he just not care?

Without saying anything else he went on through the room. Moments later Claire could hear him rummaging in the kitchen. She forced herself to stay where she was, but her heart was pounding foolishly. There was so much she'd like to say to him. A week ago she would have known how, but now he seemed so different, so distant, she was at a loss at how to approach him.

Maybe it would be best if she did give up on him and tell herself it was all for the best. But each time the idea crossed her mind, she remembered how she'd felt in his arms and the advice Liv had given her. If you have deep feelings for him, the older woman had said, don't push them or him aside.

Footsteps echoed on the hardwood floor. Claire glanced away from the television to see Madison entering the room. He stopped a couple of feet from the couch, his eyes catching hers, then sliding away. He was carrying a glass of iced water and he took a long drink before asking, ''Aren't you angry with me? Don't you want to ask me if I've been out drinking?''

Claire's eyes widened at his unexpected questions. ''It's not any of my business whether you've been out drinking or not.''

Her calmness grated on him and he wondered how she could sit there so unaffected when just the sight of her was turning him inside out. ''Your father was a drunk. Surely you hate anyone who drinks.''

She ignored his bluntness, allowing her eyes to wander up and down the long length of him. There was a leanness about him that hadn't been there before, making his arms and shoulders nothing but corded muscle. She longed to go to him, touch his face, look into his eyes and assure him that her love wouldn't hurt him. "I dislike anyone who can't drink sensibly," she corrected him. "But I don't think you've been drinking. You don't seem a bit mellow."

Her words had one corner of his mouth curling upward, although the expression held no humor. "Oh, Claire, you are the most unpredictable woman." And she did things to him, he thought with helpless anger. Without even trying, she made him want her.

"What does that mean?"

He drained the rest of the water from his glass, then placed it on the tray holding her teapot.

"Nothing," he said.

"You stayed away on purpose tonight, didn't you?" she asked.

His eyes became slits as they turned back on her. "You came down here half-naked on purpose, too, didn't you?"

Claire gasped with indignation. "You're crazy, Madison McCrea! If I wanted you to see me naked, all I'd have to do is pull this caftan over my head. And I wouldn't be bashful about doing it!"

"You probably would at that," he gritted at her.

Claire rose to her feet and utter surprise spread across his face. Any other time his expression would have made her laugh.

"Let's get one thing straight, Madison. I'm not some young virgin out to flirt with you. I'm a mature woman, one who doesn't want or need to play games."

Madison looked down at her and suddenly all the words they'd been exchanging flew out of his mind. Her dark hair tumbled around her flushed face and throat. His hands itched to reach out and tangle his fingers in its silkiness. His lips ached to taste hers. "You were playing with me this morning," he finally managed to say.

She shook her head. "No, I was merely tired of arguing with you. But what I said this morning was true. I can live without a man in my life. But that doesn't mean I want to."

Her voice lowered with the last words and her hands reached out and touched his chest. Slowly, seductively she flattened her palms against him, then slid them down and around to the small of his back.

He groaned and shook his head, but his hands reached for her shoulders. "I don't know how you can say that, Claire. I don't know how you can suddenly be so certain about things. How can a week erase all the pain you went through when you divorced?"

"It didn't erase it, Madison. It just made me see that living without you would be much more painful."

His breath sucked in as though he couldn't believe her words. "Claire, I'm not the man you think I am. I'm not the man who can make you happy. We'll both be better off when you realize that."

Her fingers tightened against his back as she drew closer, fitting herself against him.

"You can make me happy. We can make each other happy if you'd only let yourself see it."

His fingers came up and brushed against her cheek, then tunneled through her thick hair. "I don't want to hear that, Claire. It only makes it harder for me."

"You're the one who's making things hard, Madison," she murmured.

His blue eyes softened as they traveled over her face. "Holding you is the easiest thing I've ever done. Making love to you would be beautiful. But you're the kind of woman who needs more than an affair. You need a man who could build a marriage and a family with you."

It was true; she did need those things. For the past years since her divorce she'd tried to deny that she needed anything or anyone. But Madison had come along and pulled the blinders from her eyes. Her life wasn't over. She didn't want to live as if it were.

"What makes you think you're not that man? Is it me? Do you think I'm too old to give you a family?" she asked desperately.

She was the most sensuously ripe woman he'd ever known. He couldn't imagine her body incapable of conceiving and nurturing his child. "No! Damn it, Claire, I've told you before, your age has nothing to do with it!"

"It seems as if—"

Madison could no longer bear it. His head swooped down to capture her lips. He had to kiss her. He needed the smell, the feel, the taste of her to drive the torment from his mind. He didn't want to think, to reason out what was right or wrong.

He kissed her hungrily, devouring her lips as though he'd been starved for the taste of her. She felt her senses scattering, slipping further away as his plundering lips and hands worked their magic.

By the time he ended the kiss Claire was breathless and clinging to him. "I love you, Madison. Surely you know that by now," she whispered.

A shutter came down over his face and Claire could feel him pulling away, both mentally and physically. Yet she had no idea how to stop him.

"No, you don't," he said gruffly, her words causing a chilling panic inside of him. "You just think you do. After a few months with me you'd be wondering why you got yourself into another painful situation."

"Madison—"

He pulled away from her and moved to the other side of the room, as though putting several feet between them could separate them completely.

"Why, Madison? Why would I think that? Because you don't love me, is that it? You want me, but you don't love me?"

Her voice shook with emotion and the sound of it tugged Madison's head back around to her. "No, that isn't it!" he muttered fiercely.

She stepped toward him, her heart in her face. "Then tell me, Madison. I need to know what you're feeling. You say you're not a family man. I want to know why."

Anguish twisted his face as he shook his head back and forth. "You wouldn't understand, Claire."

"I think I would. Talk to me. If you don't want to talk to me as a lover, then talk to me as a friend."

"There are some men who are meant to be certain things and some who aren't. I'm not meant to be a husband or a father."

Anger surged through Claire. Quickly she closed the remaining distance between them, her head bending back as she looked determinedly up into his face. "And who told you that? Your own father?"

The color swiftly drained from his face. "Why do you say that?"

"Oh come on, Madison, I'm not stupid or blind. Every time the subject of your father comes up you close up like a locked room."

He looked away from her piercing gaze. "We don't get on, Claire. I've told you that before."

"But you haven't told me why," she insisted.

"It doesn't matter."

"It does matter!" she practically shouted. "If this is keeping us apart, it makes all the difference."

"Okay, okay," he said angrily as he began to stalk restlessly around the room. "I'm not Mitch. That's what this all boils down to. Dad wants me to be like Mitch. He always has and always will."

Her eyes traveled with him. "You hinted that before. But I thought that was only while you two were growing up."

His pacing stopped and he sank wearily down onto the couch. Claire crossed the room and took a seat a small space away from him.

"Our growing up didn't change things," Madison said, his voice so bland that Claire knew he was hiding his real feelings. "Dad always wanted me to be in oil like him and Mitch. But petroleum in any form didn't interest me. I tried to tell him that engineering was my real calling, but he always believed I went into construction to thwart him."

Suddenly Claire could see what Madison had been trying to say that day at the lake when they'd talked briefly about their childhoods. "So that's why you talked about getting loans when you first went into the business," she said with understanding. "You didn't ask your father to help you get started."

"I didn't ask. He didn't offer," Madison responded curtly.

How sad, Claire thought. She knew what it was like not to have a father's love and support. In that way she knew what Madison was feeling.

"Mitch was always the conformer," Madison spoke again, breaking into Claire's thoughts. "And I was always viewed as the rebel."

Claire smiled wanly. "Because you had a mind of your own? I don't view that as bad."

Madison snorted. "Murphy McCrea doesn't see things the way you do."

"How do you see things, Madison?" she asked softly. His hand was clenched into a fist against his thigh; she reached over and covered it with hers.

He looked at her, the mocking twist on his mouth at odds with the pain in his eyes. "I see that I could never live up to my father's expectations. I could never please him."

Claire knowingly shook her head at him. "Of course you couldn't please him. We have to live to please ourselves first before we can ever begin to please others."

"You think so," he said, his voice sardonic. "Well, Murphy McCrea would say you were selfish."

Claire's expression was grave as she studied his face. "Maybe he would. But I know, Madison. I learned the hard way. For a long time I lived to please my father and then later my husband. It didn't work for me, either.''

Madison's fist uncurled and his fingers wrapped around hers in a tight grasp. He looked unseeingly out across the room as he began to speak. ''Look, Claire, I've tried to go on with my life and put this all behind me. I've tried to tell myself it doesn't matter anymore. But I was only fooling myself. As soon as I hit Houston, it all started over again.''

''You argued with your father?'' she asked.

Madison closed his eyes as if to shut out the memory. ''When I got to the hospital and saw Mitch I— He looked so ghastly, I thought he was either going to die or be paralyzed for life. I was so angry I lashed out at Dad. I told him to take a good look at what oil had done to him and Mitch.''

''Oh Madison,'' Claire breathed as she felt the pain he must have felt at that moment, ''you didn't.''

''I did. But don't worry, you can't hurt anyone who's as tough-hided as my father. He told me in no uncertain terms that Mitch was a brave man. I was the coward for choosing a much easier and safer job.''

Claire gasped with disbelief. ''Easier! Madison—''

He shook his head, cutting in on her outrage. ''Then he went on to say that I had more or less always been a coward and chosen the easy way in life. That I'd always settled for less.''

Pent-up breath rushed out of Claire. ''And you believed him?'' she asked incredulously.

He released her hand and got to his feet. Looking down at her, he asked dryly, ''Why not, Claire? For years I tried doing the things Mitch was good at, just to try to please my father. When I continued to fall short, I quit. I decided to purposely choose directions that were easier for me."

A moment ago, Claire had been aching for him. Now she was angry all over again. "Don't you mean a direction that was right for you?"

Madison's expression was suddenly hard. But Claire ignored his anger as she rose to stand in front of him.

"No, Claire. I mean easier, safer. With Dad, it wasn't just a thing about sports, school or jobs. Murphy McCrea wanted both his sons to marry and raise families. He was a family man. He wanted his sons to be family men. So Mitch is. And he's good at it, but—"

He broke off in anguish and Claire finished for him. "But you're not a family man because you don't want to try and perhaps fall short of your brother's achievements. You don't want to take the chance of failing in your father's eyes."

Madison was actually relieved that she could finally see what was in his mind. "Right. So now you get the whole picture. I'm too much of a coward to risk trying marriage with you or anyone."

He wasn't a coward, Claire knew that better than anyone. He'd just been led to believe he was. "If you loved me, you'd be willing to risk anything."

His face suddenly softened and his hands reached out and cupped her cheeks. "I do love you, Claire. Very much. That's why I want you to have the best. You've been hurt once, you don't deserve to be hurt again."

Her heart turned over in her breast. He loved her, after all. She held onto the thought. Right now it looked as if it was all she had. Unless she fought against the walls he was putting up between them.

"How can you talk to me about loving me when all you want to do is nurse your wounded pride?"

"It's not my pride, Claire! I knew, even before I tried to explain, that you wouldn't understand!"

"I understand much more than you think. Up until now you've let your father influence every direction your life has taken—"

"That's not entirely true!" he cut in sharply, stepping away from her.

"I think it is. You're doing it now—with us. You're fighting like hell against me because ultimately you want to go against him."

Madison towered over her with dark fury. "That is certainly not true! I told you—"

"I don't care what you told me," she bit out, her anger rising to match his. "For years you've been going against him, just to show him that you're not Mitch, that you have your own identity." Some of the anger drained out of her and her eyes softened as they pleaded with him to open up to her. "To a certain degree that's good, Madison. But it's time for it to end. You're letting him—and your desire to show him you're your own man—stand between us."

He shook his head, not willing or wanting to believe the things she was saying. "And where did you get your expertise on human relations, TV talk shows?" he asked sardonically.

She simply stared at him. "Cutting me down won't change things," she said sadly.

"Cutting you! You've been standing there ripping me to shreds! I don't call that love, Claire!"

Claire couldn't stand to hear anymore. Deliberately she stepped around him and headed for the staircase. Pausing at the first step, she looked back at him. "You don't know what love is, Madison. If you did, you'd want to go to Houston and set things straight with your father. Because if you don't you'll never have a life of your own. With me or anyone else."

He snorted with disgust. "It's impossible to set things straight with Dad."

"Does that mean you won't go? You won't even give it a try for me, for us?" she asked, her voice low and desperate.

"Why should I go back there and grovel?"

Pain splintered through Claire, causing her hazel eyes to fill with tears. "Why indeed!" she choked out. "If you don't know by now, it doesn't matter anymore. I think you'd better get your things and get out."

If possible, his face grew even colder. "You're throwing me out?"

All Claire could manage to do was nod at him.

For an answer Madison brushed past her up the stairs.

Claire leaned shakily against the bannister and listened to the sound of his movements as he moved around his room.

Five minutes later she heard the front door slam and his truck engine start in the late night quiet. She was weeping openly by the time he backed onto the road and drove away.

Chapter Eleven

Three days later Claire was sitting out on the back porch. A glass of iced tea stood on the table in front of her, but it was untouched. Her chin was propped against her palm while she stared wistfully across the backyard to the mountains beyond.

It didn't surprise her that she hadn't heard from Madison since she'd thrown him out of the house. She didn't ever expect to see him again. But knowing it didn't ease the pain inside her.

The ringing of the telephone crashed into her thoughts and she forced herself to rise and go into the kitchen to answer it. When she lifted the receiver Liv's bubbly voice sounded in her ear.

"Hello, dear Claire. Did I catch you cooking supper?"

The question sent a shaft of pain through Claire. There would be no more sharing suppers with Madison. "No, I'm not in the middle of cooking. How are things with you, Liv? Have you heard from Arthur?"

"Oh yes. He's called every day."

"And . . . ? Are you any closer to working things out between you?"

"Hmm, well not in so many words. But I can tell he's missing me terribly. And I heard from one of my friends that he hasn't seen the junk dealer since I left town."

Claire wished she could say as much for Madison. "That sounds encouraging. When are you coming home? I miss you."

"I'll be back when I think the time is right. Besides, with me gone, you and Madison can have the place all to yourselves."

Tears began to collect in Claire's throat and eyes. "Madison doesn't live here anymore," she said huskily.

For once Liv was silent, then finally she said, "Claire, didn't Madison come home from Houston?"

Claire swallowed in an attempt to collect herself. "Yes, he did. His brother is going to be all right. But, well, we had some differences and I told him to leave."

"You what!"

Claire gripped the phone. "Liv, you don't understand. Madison—"

"The last time we talked, Claire, I kept telling you to hang onto the boy! Now you tell me you kicked him out! Just because he didn't call or write while he was in Houston! Well, surely, you could forgive him that!"

"Liv, it's much more serious than that," Claire tried to explain. "Madison doesn't want a relationship with me. I tried to tell you that."

Liv made a tsking sound. "Honey, I can't believe it."

"Well, you should believe it, Liv. It was probably the biggest relief of his life when I kicked him out."

Several minutes later Claire hung up. Somehow she'd managed to get Liv off the subject of Madison, but even so it hadn't helped Claire to get her mind clear of him.

She ached for him, ached to hear his voice, see his face. They'd shared such sweet, tender times together. He'd shown her how to live again, love again. But in doing so he'd hurt her.

For years since her divorce she'd told herself she would never allow herself to become close to another man, that she would never put herself into another position where she might be hurt. But the heart doesn't always listen to logic. From the moment she'd seen Madison, it had led her around as if she had no mind at all. And now she was paying dearly for it.

Claire went back out to the porch and finished her tea. While she sipped the brew, her mind kept contemplating what to do about Madison's rent money. He'd paid for six weeks and since he'd only stayed a part of that time, she had no intention of keeping his money. She had to return it to him somehow.

She'd hoped that he might think of it and come back to demand that she give him a refund. But apparently he'd not thought of it, or he had considered it worth the amount not to have to see her again.

The only thing she knew to do was drive out to the building site where McCrea Construction was erecting the new motel and give it to him in person. It wasn't something she was looking forward to, but it had to be done. First thing in the morning, she'd go, she told herself. She'd give him the money and leave. She wouldn't try to press her feelings on him in any way. No matter how badly she might want to.

After breakfast the next morning Claire dressed in white walking shorts and a red camp shirt, then headed her car toward town. Since Eureka Springs was not that large it was easy to find the building site. It was on the south outskirts of town, between a souvenir shop and a fast-food restaurant.

As Claire parked her car to one side of the highway, her eyes studied the partially erected motel. It was going to be a big structure and far grander than Madison had led her to believe. But that didn't surprise her. Madison had underplayed himself and his work. Maybe, she thought as she opened the door and stepped out, he'd underplayed his feelings for her.

Since there were several company trucks parked here and there that looked like the one Madison drove, it was impossible to tell if one of them was his.

Careful to stay out of the way, she walked around piles of lumber, brick and tar paper. Once she was closer to the working crew, she halted and searched among the group for Madison. He didn't seem to be around. After two or more sweeping glances, she decided to head for a little trailer with the word Office painted over its door.

She was halfway there when the door opened and a tall, husky man stepped out. Claire halted in her tracks as he studied her with what seemed to be amused speculation.

"Are you with the public works authority?" he asked.

Claire shook her head.

"Then I'll bet your name is Claire."

Dumbfounded, Claire stared at him. "Why yes," she finally managed to say. "How did you know?"

He gave her a broad grin. "Just a lucky guess, I suppose. I'll make another guess and say you're looking for Madison."

There was a faint twinkle in the man's eyes that made Claire wonder just exactly what he knew about her and her relationship with Madison. "Probably not for the reason you think I am."

The smile on the man's face quickly faded and he motioned for her to follow him into the trailer. "Madison isn't here now," he said.

"When will he be back?" she asked, stepping into the small office.

"Can't rightly say," Ray said. "I expect he'll call tonight and let me know. By the way, I'm Ray, Madison's foreman."

Claire turned a confused face to the man. "Do you mean . . . he's out of town?"

Ray gave a short nod. "He left early this morning for Houston. Surprised the he—heck out of me. Madison never did like that place."

More like he didn't want to face the person living there, Claire thought grimly. "Do you know why he went to Houston?" she asked, her voice growing faint as her heart began to race at a fast speed. Surely he didn't go because she'd asked him to. No, she wouldn't hope, she told herself. She'd only let herself in for more pain.

"Not really. But I have an idea it has something to do with his family." Ray went over to a small cabinet and held up a cup. "Like some coffee?" he asked her.

Claire started to refuse, then just as quickly decided it would give her a few more minutes to talk with Madison's foreman. "Yes, thank you," she told him.

He poured her a cup and motioned for her to take a seat on the couch. As she did, Ray said, "I don't know what happened with you and Madison, but it must have been pretty bad. He's been hell to live with, if you'll pardon my language, ma'am."

Claire blushed. Not because of Ray's language, but because he obviously knew that there had been something between Madison and herself. "I really doubt Madison's state of mind had anything to do with me," she said tersely.

Ray chuckled deeply as he sank down into a chair behind a small desk. "I think you're underestimating yourself, ma'am. It's been pretty obvious that Madison was smitten with you."

Claire sipped the coffee and shook her head. "At one time I had hoped so. But it's not to be." She looked at him and smiled as though the pain in her heart wasn't there at all. "Actually, I came to see Madison to return his rent money. Perhaps you could give it to him."

He shook his head. "It might get lost around here before Madison returns. Besides, I really think you should give it to him."

Claire glanced down at the the bitter coffee. "I'd rather not do that. And since he's not here anyway—"

"He'll be back," Ray said with lazy confidence.

Of course he would be back, she thought. He was the boss of this operation. But he wouldn't be back in her life. Obviously this man was a good friend, and like Liv, he wanted to see his friend happy. She felt compelled to tell him the truth of the situation. "Look, Mr.—"

"Ray," he prompted.

"Ray," she continued. "Madison doesn't want me in his life and...I don't want him in mine. At least not the way he is now. Seeing him again won't change any of that."

"Maybe. Maybe not. But Madison is a grand guy. It would be worth another try, wouldn't it?"

She let out a long sigh. "Do you know anything about his family? His father?"

The big man looked at her pointedly. "I worked as a driller for Madison's daddy long before Madison ever got into the construction business. Murphy McCrea's a shrewd businessman and he's got the wealth to prove it."

"Did you . . . like him?" Claire ventured.

Ray's laugh was dry. "As a boss? Sure. He was a fair man. But if you're asking me if he was a good father to Madison, that's something altogether different."

"They don't get on," Claire said, her voice tinged with sadness.

Ray's expression was suddenly somber. "No, they don't get on, ma'am. They're both strong-minded, I guess. Murphy's always tried to pull Madison around by the nose. I know it's because he loves his son. But if you ask me, the old man has never showed it to Madison. At least not in the right way."

"I asked him to go see his father. To try and mend the rift between them," Claire told him. "But he wouldn't."

Ray's brows lifted with speculation. "Maybe he has," he said.

Claire shook her head as she remembered how cold and hard Madison had been the last day they'd argued. She couldn't imagine him having a change of heart. "I'd rather expect he went to Houston to see about his brother."

She rose to her feet and placed the half-empty cup on the cabinet to her right. Her face was pinched with pain as she looked over at the foreman. "But you're right about one thing, Ray. Madison is a grand guy. Trouble is, he's just never realized it."

Down in Houston Madison walked through the busy airport terminal, searching for the gate where he would board his chartered flight for Eureka Springs. He wasn't looking forward to the trip, but then he wasn't really looking forward to anything, except getting out of the city and away from Murphy McCrea. For the past two days he'd tried to talk to his father, but the older man had virtually shut him out.

Now Madison knew he should have never listened to Claire, should have never come down here in hopes of setting things straight with his father. Murphy would never change and Madison was tired of trying to prove anything to his father.

Well, he would always have his engineering, he thought grimly. That was better than nothing. And he had his health. Which was more than Mitch had, who was going to have to learn how to walk all over again. But even knowing all this, Madison couldn't muster a rise in his spirits. Nothing seemed to matter now that he'd lost Claire. But hell, he would have lost her anyway, his thoughts rolled on. If he couldn't succeed at being a son, he sure wouldn't have been able to manage being a husband. Claire had been right about that.

"Madison."

A puzzled frown on his face, he looked over his shoulder at the people milling to and fro in the wide corridor. Had someone called his name? He was sure he'd heard it.

"Madison! Wait!"

This time Madison saw his father's head bobbing in and out among a crowd of people surging in his direction. The sight of the older man left Madison standing stock-still. What could have possibly sent his father rushing to find him in the airport? Another family emergency?

When Murphy drew abreast of him, Madison questioned him anxiously. "What is it? Has Mitch had a setback?"

Murphy quickly shook his head. "No, as far as I know Mitch is resting comfortably." The tall, gray-haired man grimaced as he glanced around at the travelers jostling and hurrying by them. "Can we step over here out of the way?" he asked, indicating a wall behind them where they would be out of the line of traffic.

A thousand questions whirled through Madison's mind as he joined his father. "Is Mama sick?" Madison broke in, clearly not understanding this unexpected visit from his father.

"No, damn it! No one is sick. I came here because—" His eyes suddenly slipped away from his son's face. "I wanted to speak with you before you left town."

"About what?" Madison asked in a guarded tone. For the past two days his father had wanted to do all the talking. But that hadn't surprised Madison. Murphy McCrea was not a man who liked or wanted to listen, especially where Madison was concerned.

Murphy looked his son in the eye. "About me and you."

"Dad—"

Murphy shook his head, breaking in on Madison's words. "I didn't come here to argue with you, son. I came to tell you that I've been doing some heavy thinking. Since your brother was nearly killed it's made me realize just how human we all are." He stopped and cleared his throat, then glanced away with an awkward expression on his face. "I know that I've always wanted, maybe demanded things from you that— What I'm trying to say is that I was wrong."

The stunned look on Madison's face couldn't begin to match the feelings rushing inside of him. "Did Mama send you here?" he asked suspiciously.

"She doesn't know where I am. Even though I'll admit she's been urging me to make peace with you before you left town."

"Then Mitch sent you. You're doing this to pacify him."

"Damn it, Madison, I'm doing no such thing!" Murphy roared. "You know me well enough to know that no one makes up my mind but me."

Madison said nothing as he continued to stare soberly at his father. At sixty, he was an iron-hard businessman who couldn't be patient with anyone who dared to be unlike him. Including his own son.

"Madison, is it so hard for you to believe that I love you?"

Love. Madison couldn't remember the last time he'd heard his father use that word. "I'm not the son you wanted, not like Mitch has been," he said gravely.

Murphy McCrea looked stunned. "That's not true! It angered me because you always seem to purposely defy me. I thought it was because I wasn't the father you wanted."

A soft light suddenly dawned in Madison's eyes as though he could see his father for the first time, and he could understand. After a moment he said, "I guess we've been misunderstanding each other for a long time."

Murphy's mouth twisted with a regretful smile. "It's true I used to think Mitch was the stronger of you two boys. But these past days I've had to change my mind about that, too. Mitch gave in to me when he probably shouldn't have. But you stood up to me and became your own man. That took strength of character, son. And I know it took a lot for you to come down here to Houston and tell me that. Today, as the time grew closer for you to catch your plane, I knew I couldn't let you go without telling you how I really felt. I guess we're both stubborn and proud, but I don't want that to stand between us—ever."

Murphy extended his hand to his son and Madison quickly reached for it. "Neither do I, Dad. That's why I came."

Murphy's grasp tightened on his son's hand, conveying a love that had been left unspoken for far too long. "Your mother and I will be looking for you to visit soon."

Madison nodded. "I'd like that," he said, his voice gruff with emotion. "Now I'd better catch my plane. There's a beautiful woman back in Arkansas I've missed like hell."

His father's brows lifted with faint surprise. "A woman? Are you serious about her?"

Madison smiled for the first time in days. "Very serious. Can't you see me as a family man?"

Murphy smiled broadly back at him. "Son, I can see you being anything you want to be."

Chapter Twelve

Claire aimed the hammer at the nail then swung once, twice. The nail barely budged. She swung four more times and finally the nail sunk into the yellow pine.

Six exhausting blows, she thought ruefully, when Madison could have accomplished the same feat with two or three. At this rate she'd never have the doghouse finished. Not that there was that much left to do. Today she'd almost finished with the decking on the roof. Tomorrow she'd try her hand at the shingles. She hoped by next week she'd be able to pick up the puppy she'd been promised by a friend.

Since the day she'd driven out to the construction site and talked with Madison's foreman, she'd tried to throw herself into as much work as she could find around the place, to try to keep her mind occupied. But so far it hadn't worked. Madison was in her every waking thought, and she kept wondering if he'd returned from Houston.

Several times she'd caught herself listening for his step, or looking out at the road when a vehicle approached. She knew her behavior was foolish. It was as plain as the nose on her face that Madison was gone, out of her life forever. But there was a small part of her heart that still refused to believe it.

Earlier today she'd had a surprise call from Las Vegas. It had been Liv, gushing over with happiness. From what Claire had gathered from the conversation, Arthur had gone to Illinois after Liv and when she'd refused to come back with him to Eureka Springs, he'd asked her to marry him. Now the couple was honeymooning in a motel on the Vegas strip.

Claire was very happy for her friend. Liv deserved to spend the rest of her years with the man she loved. But the news had left Claire feeling melancholy. If Liv had won Arthur over, why hadn't Claire been able to make Madison see how much they belonged together? Was she too old, or just not woman enough? The answer to those questions left her spirits at rock bottom.

"It's a good thing you're going to get that dog. Anybody could walk up on you."

Startled by the unexpected voice, Claire jerked her head up and the hammer fell from her hand. It was Madison. And her heart began to pound as he strode across the yard straight toward her.

"Madison," she said faintly, confusion pulling her brows together. "What are you doing here?"

The evening sun had long ago disappeared behind the wooded hills, filling the backyard with dusky shadows. They played across his taut features and hid the expression in his eyes as he stopped a few feet away from her. Claire felt herself holding her breath as she waited for his answer.

"I should ask what you're doing there," he replied, inclining his head to where she sat astraddle the roof of the doghouse.

"Trying my hand at carpentry," she said, while her mind raced with questions about why he'd shown up now after all this time. "I don't know what you see in it. It's hard work."

One side of his mouth cocked in a faint smile. "It's the end results that make it all worthwhile."

Claire forced herself to come down from the small building. When her legs hit the ground they felt like rubber and her palms were damp and clammy. She wiped them down the front of her jeans and said, "I suppose you came after your money. I've got it in the office if you'd like to come into the house. I attached a detailed statement to it in case you need it for your income tax."

A puzzled expression crossed his face. "Money? What are you talking about?"

He took a couple of steps toward her and Claire swallowed. He was so near, yet still so far away. "Didn't Ray tell you? I came by to return your rent money, but he said you'd gone to Houston."

"That was thoughtful of you, Claire. But I don't want your money."

He didn't seem to want anything else from her, either, she thought sadly. "You have it coming to you, and I never keep what isn't mine."

He stepped even closer, forcing Claire to bend her head back in order to look up into his face. She was trembling through and through at the thought that he might touch her, or even worse, that he might not.

"I don't want the money," he repeated.

His voice was so unyielding that Claire decided to forget the money for the moment. "I suppose you went to see your brother?"

Madison nodded. "I saw him while I was there," he said. They were so close he could feel the heat of her body, smell the flowery scent of her skin. It was all he could do to keep from reaching out for her. And the only thing holding him back was the fear that she might not be willing to forgive him, or that she might no longer want him.

"And how was he?" she asked, unaware that her voice had a breathy sound to it.

"Improving."

She nervously licked her lips, then wished she hadn't when he turned his eyes upon them. "That's good," she managed to say.

"Has Liv come home?"

This was ridiculous, she thought. No one stood this close just to have small talk. She wanted to move away but found it impossible to make her legs work. He was like a magnet drawing her ever closer. "No. Liv is in Las Vegas. Honeymooning," she added.

His brows lifted with surprise, then suddenly he was laughing. "You mean old Arthur finally caved in?"

Claire wanted to be angry with him for such a macho statement, but his laughter made him sound like the old Madison she'd first fallen in love with, making it impossible to scold him. "If you mean did he marry her, yes. They seem very happy," she tacked on.

"That's good. But I guess that means you lose a renter."

Claire shook her head. "No. Arthur will be moving in with Liv. They both think they'll like living in my house."

"I liked living in your house," he commented softly.

Claire drew in a sharp breath as she searched his face. "Why are you here, Madison?"

His hands were reaching for her even before she finished the question. "To see if you're willing to forgive me."

It was the last thing she'd expected him to say and the shock nearly buckled her knees. "I—why should it matter?"

His hands gently kneaded her shoulders as his eyes looked deeply into hers. "Because I love you, Claire."

She looked at him for long moments and then suddenly a sob shook her throat. "Oh Madison," she groaned. "I've missed you so."

He pressed her head tightly against his chest as his fingers threaded themselves into her silky hair. "Not nearly as much as I've missed you, darlin' Claire," he whispered against the top of her head.

"But Madison, why? When you left here—"

"A lot has happened since I left here, Claire. And among the very first was that I knew I was going to be miserable without you."

She tilted her head back in order to look up at him. "But you were so adamant about not marrying, and—"

He shook his head. "I know I hurt you, Claire. But believe me when I tell you I was only acting that way because I loved you so much. I knew you were worthy of the best. I wanted to be able to give you the best. I wanted to be a man you would be proud of, one who could fulfill every part of your life. But I'd tried so many times in the past to do the same with my father and had ended up failing. I knew it would kill me if I tried and failed with you."

"Oh, Madison," she whispered tearfully. "I don't expect you to be perfect. Neither one of us will ever be perfect. I just want you to love me."

"I do. I will," he vowed fervently while hugging her even closer to him. "Oh, Claire, I was so miserable without you I knew I had to do something. I went to Houston in a last desperate attempt to right things with Dad."

"I didn't want you to grovel, Madison. I never wanted that. I just wanted you to stand up to him. Tell him that you must live your own life with or without his blessing."

"I didn't grovel," he told her, then his mouth curved with amusement. "I think I more or less growled. And when I was through growling I thought it had gone like it always had in the past—to a dead-end street. I was at the airport getting ready to catch my flight to come back here when Dad showed up."

Claire leaned away from him, her eyes wide with surprise as she gazed up at him. "What did he say?"

Madison grinned down at her. "Actually he said a lot, but the crux of it was that he loved me. And I realized that was all I'd ever really needed to hear from him."

His blue eyes were lit with a joy that weaved its way into Claire's heart. She smiled at him as happiness bubbled up inside of her. "I'm so glad for you, Madison."

"You were right, Claire," he said, his hands reaching up to gently cup her cheeks. "Once I settled things with Dad everything fell into place, and I knew that loving you, marrying you wasn't going to be a risk at all."

She breathed his name, but it was all she had time to get out before his face bent down to hers and his lips took hers in a kiss so sweetly consuming it left her dizzy.

"Does this mean you're going to finish my doghouse?" she asked teasingly.

A sly, sexy grin spread across his face. "Claire, you remember what happened the last time we worked on the doghouse."

She slanted him a provocative glance beneath her lashes. "How could I forget? You're a dangerous man to be around, Madison McCrea."

Laughing, he reached down and swept her up in his arms. "I wasn't talking about squashing your finger, Claire."

Her happy giggles sounded in the night air as he carried her into the house and up the staircase.

*   *   *   *   *

WRITTEN IN THE STARS

Travel along with
THE MAN FROM NATCHEZ
by Elizabeth August

When a lovely lady waves a red flag to tempt the Taurus man, will the bullheaded hunk charge into romance...or be as stubborn as ever? Find out in May in THE MAN FROM NATCHEZ by Elizabeth August...the fifth book in our Written in the Stars series!

Rough and rugged farmer Nate Hathaway wasn't about to let Stacy Jamison go it alone while searching for treasure in the Shenandoah Mountains! The man from Natchez was about to embark on a very tempting trip....

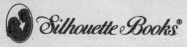

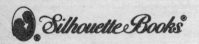

Take 4 bestselling love stories FREE

Plus get a FREE surprise gift!

Special Limited-time Offer

Mail to **Silhouette Reader Service®**

In the U.S.
3010 Walden Avenue
P.O. Box 1867
Buffalo, N.Y. 14269-1867

In Canada
P.O. Box 609
Fort Erie, Ontario
L2A 5X3

YES! Please send me 4 free Silhouette Romance® novels and my free surprise gift. Then send me 6 brand-new novels every month, which I will receive months before they appear in bookstores. Bill me at the low price of $2.25* each. There are no shipping, handling or other hidden costs. I understand that accepting the books and gift places me under no obligation ever to buy any books. I can always return a shipment and cancel at any time. Even if I never buy another book from Silhouette, the 4 free books and the surprise gift are mine to keep forever.

*Offer slightly different in Canada—$2.25 per book plus 69¢ per shipment for delivery. Sales tax applicable in N.Y. Canadian residents add applicable federal and provincial sales tax.

215 BPA HAYY (US)   315 BPA 8176 (CAN)

Name _____ (PLEASE PRINT)

Address _____ Apt. No. _____

City _____ State/Prov. _____ Zip/Postal Code _____

This offer is limited to one order per household and not valid to present Silhouette Romance® subscribers. Terms and prices are subject to change.

SROM-BPADR   © 1990 Harlequin Enterprises Limited

IT'S A CELEBRATION OF MOTHERHOOD!

Following the success of BIRDS, BEES and BABIES, we are proud to announce our second collection of Mother's Day stories.

to Mother with Love

THREE ROMANTIC STORIES CELEBRATING MOTHERHOOD

LINDA HOWARD
ROBYN CARR
CHERYL REAVIS

Three stories in one volume, all by award-winning authors—stories especially selected to reflect the love all families share.

Available in May, TO MOTHER WITH LOVE is a perfect gift for yourself or a loved one to celebrate the joy of motherhood.

Silhouette Books®

ML-1